BLAST FRO

"Who is it?" Carole a   phone.

Colonel Hanson winked. "You'll just have to wait and find out for yourself."

Carole put the phone to her ear. "Hello?" she said uncertainly.

"Hi, Carole," the voice on the other end of the line replied. A strangely familiar voice, but one that Carole couldn't quite place. "Guess who?"

"Umm . . ." Carole searched her mind desperately. It was a male voice, young—but who? The answer tugged at the corners of her memory, but she couldn't quite grasp it.

The voice laughed. "Guess that isn't really fair, but I couldn't resist putting you on the spot. It's Cam."

"Cam?" Carole repeated blankly. Suddenly she gasped. "Cam! Is that really you?"

**Don't miss any of the excitement
at PINE HOLLOW,
where friends come first:**

PINE HOLLOW®

HIGH STAKES

BY BONNIE BRYANT

BANTAM BOOKS
NEW YORK · TORONTO · LONDON · SYDNEY · AUCKLAND

Special thanks to Laura Roper of Sir "B" Farms

RL: 5.0, AGES 012 AND UP

HIGH STAKES
A Bantam Book/August 2000

ISBN: 0-553-49303-5

Visit us on the Web! www.randomhouse.com
Educators and librarians, for a variety of teaching tools, visit us at
www.randomhouse.com/teachers

Published simultaneously in the United States and Canada

Bantam Books is an imprint of Random House Children's Books, a division
of Random House, Inc. BANTAM BOOKS and the rooster colophon
are registered trademarks of Random House, Inc. Bantam Books, 1540
Broadway, New York, New York 10036.

PRINTED IN THE UNITED STATES OF AMERICA

OPM   10 9 8 7 6 5 4 3 2 1

*My special thanks to Catherine Hapka
for her help in the writing of this book.*

ONE

"Do you think Mom and Dad would kill me if I came home with another dog?" Stevie Lake asked, stopping in front of a roomy cage where a medium-sized black-and-white dog was leaping against the wire door, panting and whining eagerly at her.

"Yes," Lisa Atwood replied with a smile. "I think they probably would."

Stevie sighed. "Yeah, you're right," she agreed, putting her palm against the wire so the excited dog could sniff at it. "I can already hear them: 'Sure, Stevie, the dog can stay. He can have your room.' Then I'd be here at CARL myself, hoping some nice family would come and take me home. And somehow, I don't think most people would consider a sixteen-year-old girl the perfect family pet. Not even a totally wonderful and talented one like me."

Lisa grinned, her grayish blue eyes twinkling. "Come on. I smell paint up ahead. Let's go find Carole."

1

"Okay." With one last glance at the friendly dog, Stevie followed her friend down the wide hallway. On either side of her were more cages, almost all of them occupied. Dogs of every shape and size pressed themselves eagerly against the wire or barked as the girls walked by.

"Wow," Lisa commented, raising her voice to make herself heard over the racket. Pushing back her straight blond hair, she covered her ears with her hands. "And I thought my old dog, Dolly, could be noisy sometimes!"

Stevie didn't answer. In fact, she'd barely heard her friend's comment. She was staring at a dog that had just come in from the outdoor run that adjoined its pen. "Check it out!" she exclaimed sorrowfully, hurrying forward for a better look. "This one looks just like Bear!" She could hardly believe how much the strange dog resembled her family's golden retriever, despite the fact that this dog's silky coat was badly in need of a brushing. However, when she took a step forward, pressing her hand to the wire as she'd done with the black-and-white dog, Stevie saw that there was another difference as well. Instead of racing forward to get acquainted like the other dog had, or ambling slowly over for a lazy sniff, as Bear would have done, this dog hung back warily. Its fringed tail wagged hesitantly a couple of times, then it backed away and ducked through the door to the outside run again.

Lisa was watching. "Sad," she said quietly. "Looks like it wants to make friends, but it's too scared to try."

"Hey! There you are," a familiar voice said from the end of the hall. "I was wondering why the dogs were barking all of a sudden."

Glancing up, Stevie saw Carole Hanson smiling at them, a paintbrush in her hand and a smudge of pale yellow paint just above one dark brown eye. Dressed in baggy overalls and a red turtleneck, her springy black curls pulled back into a loose braid at the nape of her neck, she looked downright adorable. Stevie didn't say so, though—Carole could be shy about taking compliments, especially ones regarding her appearance. "Hey, we told you we'd stop by and help out," Stevie commented instead. "So here we are, ready and willing."

"Come on back." Carole gestured to the room behind her. "Most of the group's outside raking the paddock, but a few of us are getting started on the playroom."

"The playroom?" Stevie wrinkled her brow. She'd been to the County Animal Rescue League—a local shelter commonly known as CARL—several times before, but not recently. "What's that? Don't tell me they keep stray kids here, too. I thought I was kidding about that." She shot Lisa a wry smile.

Carole laughed. "Nope. But listening to all the stories people have about this place, it sounds like they've had just about every other kind of critter at one time or another. Even horses."

"I know," Lisa said, biting her lip. "There was a horse here the first time we ever came. Remember?"

Stevie nodded. She had never actually seen the horse Lisa was talking about, but she still remembered how upset her friend had been when the poor, abused animal had died despite the best efforts of the volunteer vets at CARL. *We were all upset,* Stevie thought, glancing from one of her best friends to the other. *But what else would you expect from the three horse-crazy girls we were then?* She smiled slightly. *Not that we're really that different today, when you get right down to it.* It was their common love of horses and riding that had brought the three of them together in the first place back in junior high. Now that they were in high school—Stevie and Carole were juniors; Lisa was a senior—they were as close as ever. Maybe they didn't spend quite as much time hanging out at Pine Hollow Stables as they once had, but horses were still a very important part of their lives.

That was especially true of Carole. Of the three of them, she had always been the most serious about horses and riding. Up until recently, Carole had still spent every moment she could at the stable. She'd even taken a part-time job as stable hand. But all that had changed when Carole, who was normally one of the most honest and straightforward people Stevie knew, had cheated on a test at school. That had been enough to get her grounded for more than a month—no phone calls, no TV, and most important of all, no riding. Stevie had been as surprised as everyone else when Carole's father, Colonel Hanson, had partially lifted that ban because Carole had scored very well on the PSATs. Now she was allowed to ride a few times per week, but the rest of the punishment still stood.

"So this is the playroom, huh?" Stevie said as Carole led the way into a small square room just beyond the dog area. Stevie glanced around curiously. Two men in their late twenties were in the doorway on the opposite side, carefully marking off the door frame with masking tape. "You still haven't told us what it's for."

"Duh," Lisa commented, gesturing to a couple of wire exercise pens that had been folded up and stacked against the far wall. "It must be where people can come to get acquainted with the animals they're thinking about adopting. Right?" She glanced at Carole for confirmation.

Carole nodded. "You got it. People can bring a dog or cat in and hang out for a while to see if it's the pet for them. It's quieter and more peaceful than the holding rooms, so it's easier to get to know each other in here."

"Oh, yeah." Stevie shrugged sheepishly. "I guess

that is kind of obvious. But hey, I haven't been here in a long time. Just call me Ms. Short-Term Memory."

"That's exactly why CARL has its holiday fundraiser party every December," Carole said, dipping her paintbrush into a large can of yellow paint. As a further condition of her punishment, Carole had been spending most of her free time lately volunteering with Hometown Hope, a group that fixed up run-down houses and other buildings and sometimes built new houses for poor families. That week they were sprucing up the grounds and buildings at CARL. "I mean, it's not just a fun way to raise money. It's also a way to remind people in the community that the shelter is here, and that it can use their help and support all year long."

"Wow." Stevie shot Carole a sidelong glance. "You really have been talking to people here, haven't you? You're practically a professional CARL cheerleader."

"It's a great cause," Carole said, blushing slightly as she started brushing paint onto the narrow space between the door and the adjacent wall. "I guess I can get kind of worked up about it sometimes."

Lisa smiled. "Kind of. But we understand."

Stevie watched as Lisa grabbed a paint pan and carefully poured some of the yellow paint into it. "Too bad I won't get to write that article about the fund-raiser," she muttered. "You could have helped me a lot with my research." A couple of weeks earlier

Stevie had joined the staff of her school newspaper, the Fenton Hall *Sentinel*. So far she'd had the chance to write a couple of interesting articles, but as a new reporter, she was pretty much last in line when it came to the really juicy assignments. When Carole had told her about the CARL fund-raiser the afternoon before, Stevie had been so sure that the story was her ticket to the front page that she'd called the editor, Theresa Cruz, at home to tell her about it. She still couldn't believe what Theresa's response had been. *Sorry, Stevie,* the editor had told her briskly. *You're a little late. Mary Zane came up with the same idea back in November.*

"That *is* too bad," Carole agreed, bending down to pick a piece of lint out of the paint can. "You would have done a great job, Stevie."

Lisa rolled her eyes. "Don't encourage her, Carole, please," she begged in mock dismay as she picked up a roller and started spreading yellow paint over the white primer on the wall. "The whole drive over here, all I heard about was how unfair it was that another reporter gets to do *her* big story. Never mind that this all happened, like, weeks before Stevie even decided to join the school paper in the first place."

Stevie frowned, reaching for the second roller to help with the painting. "Very funny," she said. "It *is* unfair. Mary doesn't even have any pets. What does she know about an animal shelter?"

"You're still coming to the fund-raiser, though,

7

aren't you?" Carole asked anxiously. "I mean, I know I only got two free tickets, but—"

"Don't worry," Stevie interrupted, smiling at the worried look on her friend's face. "I'm still coming. And you and Lisa can use those tickets. Phil and I don't mind paying for ours. The price is kind of steep, but our parents already said they'd help out if we're a little short. And it's all for a good cause, right?"

"Carole?" one of the young men broke into their conversation, walking over at that moment. "We just finished taping off the doors. Can you and your friends handle the painting for a little while? Jay and I haven't had a lunch break yet."

"Sure, Louis," Carole replied. "We'll be fine. Have a good lunch."

When the three girls were alone, Stevie cleared her throat and glanced at Lisa. She'd been thinking about something ever since the topic of the fund-raiser had come up—and it didn't have anything to do with the *Sentinel*. "So, Lisa," she said hesitantly. "Um, I was just wondering. Er, it sounds like this fund-raiser is going to be kind of, um . . . Well, it sounds like there will be dancing and stuff. So I was just wondering if you were planning to, you know, ask anybody. As a date."

Lisa shot her a quick, unreadable glance. Then she shrugged. "I don't think so," she replied. "I know Alex and I are supposed to see other people—that's what we agreed to do—but it's kind of soon."

8

Stevie tried not to let her relief show. Lisa had been dating Stevie's twin brother, Alex, for the better part of a year. Just a few days earlier, the two of them had decided to take a break from their relationship and see other people for a while. Stevie still wasn't sure she understood why—she couldn't imagine ever wanting to take a break from her boyfriend, Phil Marsten, even though they'd been together much longer than Lisa and Alex had. As far as Stevie was concerned, it was kind of silly for two people who cared about each other to choose *not* to be together.

"I hear you," she said casually, not wanting Lisa to guess what she was thinking. "Still, maybe you just need to jump right in and do it. Why not ask a guy you like as a friend? I mean, not every date has to be some huge romantic thing, right? You could just ask someone as, like, a buddy thing. Say, someone like Scott."

"Scott?" Carole put in, looking surprised. "You think Lisa should ask Scott out?"

"Sure," Stevie replied. "Why not? He's a nice guy, right? Not bad-looking. Totally presentable." She smiled blandly. Scott Forester and his sister, Callie, had moved to Willow Creek the previous summer. Their father was a congressman who commuted from the peaceful small town to nearby Washington, D.C. Callie had been a junior endurance champion in her old hometown on the West Coast, so Stevie and her friends had adopted her into their group almost immediately. Then one rainy night over the summer, Stevie, Carole, and Callie had been involved in a serious car accident, which had left Callie unable to walk without crutches for many months. Right after the accident, Scott had been very angry with Stevie, blaming her for his sister's problems, since she'd been driving the car. But eventually he had seen that no one was at fault, and before long Stevie could hardly imagine a time when she and Scott hadn't been friends.

"Scott?" Lisa repeated dubiously, pausing in her painting long enough to tuck her hair behind her ear and glance at Stevie. "I don't know. I mean, I like Scott and everything, but it's not like we're best friends. If I wanted to ask any guy on a friendly date like you're talking about, I'd probably ask someone like A.J."

Stevie frowned. "A.J.?" she said. "Forget A.J. Scott would make a way better date. I mean, A.J.'s, like, *short*."

Lisa looked surprised. "So what if he's short? What do you have against A.J. all of a sudden?" she demanded.

"Nothing." Stevie grinned weakly, realizing she might be coming off as obnoxious. Maybe even a little psychotic. After all, A.J. McDonnell was Phil's best friend of many years, and Stevie had always been crazy about him. "A.J.'s cool. I was just, um, kidding."

"I think it's a great idea," Carole put in, glancing over from her work near the door. "Why don't you ask A.J., Lisa? You'll still have the free ticket, so each of you would only need to come up with half the price of a ticket."

"Wait!" Stevie exclaimed, feeling rather desperate. The conversation was rapidly rolling out of her control. "Forget A.J. What about Scott?"

"What about him?" Lisa asked, cocking an eyebrow at her. "What's with you, Stevie? Why are you suddenly so hyped to hook me up with Scott?"

Stevie realized there was no point keeping her problem from her best friends. Maybe they could even help her figure out a way to deal with it. Feeling sheepish, she took a deep breath. "Okay, I might as well tell you guys. I think Scott might, um, like me. You know—as in *like* like me."

"Huh?" Carole shot her a suspicious look. "I don't get it. What's the punch line?"

"This isn't a joke!" Stevie protested. "I mean it, I think Scott has a crush on me. Haven't you noticed the way he always seems to be hanging around Pine Hollow lately? At first it made sense, since he had to drive Callie around everywhere. But her leg is all better now—she could easily walk to Pine Hollow from their house, so there's no reason for him to be there all the time, since he doesn't even ride."

Lisa looked pensive. "Hey, you know, you're right," she said. "I hadn't really thought much about

11

it, but Scott does hang out at the stable a lot." She grinned. "Still, what makes you think you have anything to do with it? Maybe he just secretly dreams of joining the beginners' class."

"Yeah, right," Stevie replied sarcastically. "Or maybe he's hooked on the smell of manure. Come on, guys. It's not like Scott couldn't find something better to do with his time. He's not exactly Mr. Shy and Lonely, in case you hadn't noticed." That was an understatement, and Stevie knew it. Scott had inherited his politician father's gift for connecting with people and making friends. "So why would he start spending all his spare time at Pine Hollow for no apparent reason?"

"Okay, that's a point," Carole said diplomatically. "But seriously, Stevie, what makes you think he's interested in you? Not that you're not, like, totally lovable and all, of course." She grinned. "But like you said, Scott's no pathetic Mr. Lonely Heart. And he knows about Phil."

Stevie shrugged. "I know. But he's always, you know, talking to me and saying hi in the halls at school and stuff. Um, and we did spend a lot of time together when he was running for student body president a while back." She paused and bit her lip. When she said it out loud, it really didn't sound like much to go on. Carole and Lisa were both students at the public high school in town, so they had no way of knowing what went on at Fenton Hall, the private school that Stevie and the Foresters attended. "Come on, though," she insisted. "Evidence or not, I'm not imagining things here. Really. You know how it is—you can always sort of tell when a guy is into you. It's just a weird sort of feeling, right?"

"Sure," Lisa said immediately. "I know what you mean."

Carole shrugged. "I don't," she admitted. "You guys are the experts when it comes to this stuff, I guess."

Stevie shot her a quick glance. A few days earlier Carole had confided to her and Lisa that she was interested in Ben Marlow, one of the stable hands at Pine Hollow. Stevie hadn't been totally surprised—she had noticed for a while now that Carole got kind of tongue-tied and confused when the topic turned to Ben—but that didn't mean she was happy about it. Carole wasn't very experienced when it came to guys and dating, and Ben was a difficult case, to say the least. The brooding young stable hand seemed determined to maintain a wall of coolness and suspicion between himself and the world, and Stevie didn't want Carole to run up against that wall and get hurt. "Well, anyway, Lisa," she said, "it would make me feel better if you could get Scott to focus on someone else for a while. Specifically, someone like you."

Lisa looked unconvinced. "I don't know, Stevie," she said slowly. "I'd love to help you out, but I'm just not sure I'm ready to ask anyone out on a date yet. Even a platonic friend like Scott."

"Oh." Stevie was disappointed, but she knew better than to push it. She could tell Lisa's mind was made up. "Okay, if you're sure you don't want to go with a date, I guess I can understand that."

"The only person I can imagine going with right now is Carole." Lisa grinned at her friend. "So how about it? Want to be my date?"

"I'd be honored," Carole replied with a giggle. "It's a date."

Stevie rolled her eyes and sighed. Still, she couldn't really be upset about Lisa's decision. *Maybe this means I still have to figure out what to do about Scott,* she thought, turning her attention back to her painting as Lisa and Carole started chatting about the fund-raiser. *But at least there's a definite bright side. If Lisa can't even stand the thought of one date with another guy, maybe that means she and Alex will be back together even sooner than I expected.*

Carole hit the spell-check command on her computer, sat back in her desk chair, and stretched. *Whew,* she thought. *I can't believe I'm almost finished. Thank goodness—once this paper is behind me, maybe I'll feel like this whole stupid incident is behind me, too.*

She glanced around her room, her gaze lingering briefly on the framed photo on the table beside her bed. The snapshot showed her horse, Starlight, leaning his big bay head on her shoulder as the two of

14

them stood in Pine Hollow's back paddock. It was one of Carole's favorite photos, because it captured the gelding's gentle, curious personality perfectly. She also loved it because, to her, it summed up the reasons she loved horses and planned to dedicate her life to them. Some people didn't understand how she could feel that way, but to Carole, planning her life around horses was as natural as breathing.

Then again, some people do understand, she thought, an image of Ben popping into her mind. *At least I think they do. About how I feel about horses, if nothing else . . .*

She sighed, wondering why thinking about Ben always made her feel so mixed up and anxious. Why did things between them have to be so complicated? She wondered what it would be like to know how he felt about her. To know for sure that he cared about her as much as she did about him, to be in a real relationship with him—a romance, just like her friends had with their boyfriends—instead of always having to wonder if he even liked her at all.

It would be nice if Ben could act more like a regular guy sometimes, she thought wistfully. *Then maybe we would already be, well—we could be making plans to go to the CARL fund-raiser together. Like on a real date.* She could picture it now: The two of them would meet at the stable for a quick ride. Then they would change into nice clothes and drive over to CARL, where they would dance for a while, then slip away to visit with the animals in the shelter and steal a little private time . . .

She blushed, banishing the image almost as soon as it came. Maybe, just maybe, things were starting to look sort of interesting between her and Ben. They were talking again, and Ben had even shared a few things about himself and his past. That was a pretty rare occurrence, and Carole couldn't help taking it as a sign that he thought she was special, at least a little. But it was a big leap from there to being an actual couple, dancing and going out on dates and hanging out with their friends at the pizza place or the mall.

Carole sighed. She couldn't imagine that. *Ben at the mall?* she thought wryly. *Yeah, right. That will happen at about the same time Starlight starts doing my algebra homework for me.*

Thinking of homework reminded her of what she was supposed to be doing. Focusing on the computer screen, she saw that it was blinking the word *hitsory* at her. With a grimace, Carole corrected it to *history.* Then she tapped the key to continue the spell-check search.

I guess maybe that's my problem, she thought. *If I can't even imagine being with Ben, how is it ever going to happen?* She frowned slightly. *I mean, if Stevie liked a guy, she would probably just march right up to him and ask him out. Why can't I do that? I may tell myself it's because it would scare Ben too much, but is that really it? Or is it that it would scare* me *too much?*

16

She didn't like that thought. But what could she do? There was no way she was going to turn herself into Stevie. What would she do—walk up to Ben, tap him on the shoulder, and say, "Hey, good-looking. Want to be my hot date this Friday night?"

Suddenly remembering something Stevie had said earlier that day, Carole sat up straight in her chair. *Still, who says it has to be some big romantic date?* she thought. *There's no law that says I can't invite Ben to come along to the CARL thing just as a friend. After all, he loves animals, right? He would probably think this is as great a cause as I do. And I could give him my free ticket. I'm sure if I explained that Ben doesn't have any money, Dad would buy me another one. . . .*

She actually wasn't sure about that at all. While her father might not mind making a donation to CARL, he had been a little skeptical about her request to attend the fund-raiser. He'd agreed after some pleading, but Carole definitely didn't want to test that decision too much.

Well, maybe Lisa could hit up her dad for money for the third ticket, she thought uncertainly. *Ever since the divorce, he buys her just about anything she wants. That way Ben and I could use the free tickets, and everything would be cool.*

"How's it going, honey?" Carole's father's voice interrupted her thoughts.

Glancing over, she saw him standing in the doorway to her room. "Pretty good," she replied, quickly

17

returning her attention to the computer. "I want to read through it one more time, but I think I'm just about done." Her history teacher had assigned the research paper as a way for Carole to help make up for cheating on that test, and Colonel Hanson had been following his daughter's progress closely.

"Good." Colonel Hanson smiled, looking pleased. "Do you have time for a quick snack break? I just made popcorn."

"Sure." Carole had had a very close relationship with her father ever since her mother had died when Carole was younger. They had become almost as much friends as just father and daughter. But their friendship had been on rocky ground after the truth came out about what had happened during that history test. It had only improved once Carole had really figured out just why her father was so upset and owned up to what she'd done without trying to make excuses.

Of course, that's nothing to the turnaround in Dad's mood since those PSAT scores came, Carole thought as she followed her father down the stairs. *Dad acts like acing that one test was more awesome than winning the Grand National and making the U.S. Equestrian Team all rolled into one.*

Soon the two of them were sitting at the kitchen table, glasses of cold soda and a large bowl of buttery popcorn between them. "I'm glad you're taking this make-up assignment seriously, sweetheart," Colonel Hanson said, reaching into the bowl and grabbing a generous handful of popcorn. "I'm proud of you."

"Thanks." Carole took a sip of her soda.

"Not just for finishing your paper early," Colonel Hanson went on. "I'm also proud of the way you've learned from your mistake. You're really doing a great job of getting your life back in balance."

"What do you mean?" Carole asked uncertainly, glancing up with her hand halfway to the popcorn bowl.

Her father smiled fondly at her. "I mean, I've always been proud of you for how hard you work at your riding and at taking such good care of Starlight, you know that. But now, I really like seeing you putting your best efforts into other things, too. You've been doing a terrific job with Hometown Hope— your vice principal raved about what a hard worker you are when I ran into her at the supermarket a couple of days ago. And don't think I haven't noticed the way you've been throwing yourself into getting CARL ready for their fund-raiser—I know it's not just because you're looking forward to the party, either." He smiled and winked as he reached for a napkin to wipe the butter off his fingers. "I've also been noticing that your homework has been getting done well ahead of time lately, and I'm sure your next report card is going to reflect your efforts to do better on your schoolwork. And of course, there are your PSAT scores—I'm especially glad that you took that test seriously enough to do so well on it. If you do that well on the SATs in the spring, it will mean a lot of exciting choices for your future."

Carole took a few pieces of popcorn and tossed them into her mouth, chewing busily to keep herself from having to answer for a moment. She wasn't sure how to feel about what her father was saying. On the one hand, she was always happy when he was pleased with her. However, it almost sounded like he was saying she was better off focusing on stuff outside the stable, which didn't make sense to her at all.

He knows how much horses mean to me, she thought, feeling a little confused. *He knows I want to spend my life working with them. How are the SATs going to affect that, really? All I need to do is score well enough to get into a decent school with a good equine studies program, not win a Rhodes scholarship or something.*

Still, maybe he just needed a little gentle reminder. "That reminds me, Dad," she said tentatively. "Um, speaking of the future, I've been meaning to tell you, I've been spending a lot of time lately thinking about what I want to do when I finish school."

"Oh?" Colonel Hanson grabbed the salt shaker and added a few shakes to the bowl. "That's nice, sweetie. But I don't think you need to start worrying about it too much just yet. You've still got a year and a half of high school to go, and you'll have plenty of time to figure out what you want to do while you're in college getting a good, solid liberal arts education to start you off right."

This time Carole could hardly believe her ears. What was her father trying to say? She'd never hidden the fact that she wanted to major in equine studies in college, just as Denise McCaskill, the stable manager at Pine Hollow, had done. But her father seemed to have forgotten all about that. Did he really think she was going to spend four years in college just for the sake of studying the same dull stuff she was learning in high school?

Before she could figure out how to respond, the phone rang. "I'll get it," Colonel Hanson said cheerfully, licking his fingers and hopping out of his chair to grab the phone off the counter. "Hello?" he said into the receiver.

Carole was so bewildered by her father's comments about her future that she hardly noticed what he was saying into the phone until she heard him mention her name. She glanced up curiously and saw that he was smiling broadly, looking like a cat who had just swallowed a particularly tasty stable rat.

Who could that be? she wondered distractedly. *He wouldn't be looking so surprised if it was just Stevie or someone. Maybe it's one of our relatives calling from Minnesota.*

"Of course, she's right here," her father was telling

the person on the other end of the line. "I'm sure she'd love to talk with you. I'm afraid you'll have to keep it short, though—she's supposed to be grounded. Normally she's not allowed to take phone calls at all, but I'll make an exception since this is a very special case."

"Who is it?" Carole asked as he held out the phone.

Her father winked. "You'll just have to wait and find out for yourself."

More puzzled than ever, Carole put the phone to her ear. "Hello?" she said uncertainly.

"Hi, Carole," the voice on the other end of the line replied. A strangely familiar voice, but one that Carole couldn't quite place. "Guess who?"

"Umm . . ." Carole searched her mind desperately. It was a male voice, young—but who? The answer tugged at the corners of her memory, but she couldn't quite grasp it.

The voice laughed. "Guess that isn't really fair, but I couldn't resist putting you on the spot. It's Cam."

"Cam?" Carole repeated blankly. Suddenly she gasped. "Cam! Is that really you?"

More laughter bubbled through the phone. "It's me," Cam said, sounding amused and delighted. "Surprised?"

"Totally!" Carole couldn't believe it. She hadn't heard from Cam Nelson for years. Way back in junior high, the two of them had met at a horse show and become good friends, and maybe even a little more—Carole had invited Cam to a few dances and parties and other events at Pine Hollow, and he had even become an honorary member of a group that Carole and her best friends had formed, which they'd called The Saddle Club. Carole had often wondered what might have happened if Cam's family hadn't moved to Los Angeles a few years earlier. Maybe if he'd been around for the past few years, Carole wouldn't have been the only one of her friends who had never had a serious boyfriend. Maybe she wouldn't have felt so left out when Stevie and Lisa talked about relationship problems or where their boyfriends would be taking them on Saturday night. Maybe she wouldn't have had to wonder what a real romance was like. . . .

"Carole?" Cam said, interrupting her thoughts. "Are you still there? You didn't faint or anything, did you?"

"I'm here," Carole replied quickly, realizing that she had been silent for several seconds. "Conscious and everything. I'm just kind of stunned, I guess."

"In a good way, I hope," Cam said lightly. "This is supposed to be a *good* surprise."

"Oh, it is!" Carole assured him hastily. "Really. I—I just can't believe it's you. Where are you calling from?"

"That's the best part," Cam replied. "I'm calling from right here in Virginia. Fifteen Strawberry Hill Lane, to be exact."

Carole wrinkled her forehead, confused. "What do you mean?" she asked. "Isn't that your old address over in Arden Hills? Are you visiting your old house?"

Cam laughed. "Nope. We moved back! My dad got transferred back to D.C., and when my folks called the real estate agent, they found out our old place was up for sale. It was fate!" He cleared his throat and lowered his voice. "Just like I think it may be fate that I'm moving back here, close to you."

Carole wasn't sure how to respond to that. "Oh," she said lamely. "Um, this is such a surprise! I can't believe you really moved back."

"Me either. The best part is, you're still here, too. I can't wait to see you again. So when can we get together?"

"Oh," Carole said again. "Um, like my dad said, I'm sort of grounded right now. I don't think I—" Noticing that her father was waving for her attention from his seat at the kitchen table, Carole cut herself off. "Could you hold on a sec?"

"As long as you need," Cam replied promptly.

Carole covered the mouthpiece with her hand. "What is it, Dad?"

"Pardon me for eavesdropping, sweetie," Colonel

Hanson said with a smile. "But can I deduce that young Cam wants to see you?"

Carole nodded. "Don't worry. I was just about to tell him it'll have to wait until after New Year's." That was when her grounding ended.

"Well, I think we might be able to make an exception," her father said, still smiling. "After all, this is a special case. Go ahead and tell Cam you can meet him tomorrow afternoon if he likes—*after* you finish your work with Hometown Hope."

Carole couldn't believe her ears. Her father had been a member of the Marine Corps for many years before his recent retirement, and even though he was an easygoing person most of the time, he did believe in discipline. Carole couldn't remember the last time he'd gone back on a punishment, and now he had done it twice—first letting her ride again because of her PSAT scores, and now this. "Really?" she asked, just to make sure she hadn't misunderstood. "I can see Cam tomorrow?"

"Yes," Colonel Hanson said. "I always liked Cam. I'm glad that he's moved back to the area." He winked. "And I think it would be cruel and unusual punishment to make you wait weeks to see him. So go ahead, have fun."

"Thanks, Dad!" Carole uncovered the phone. "Cam? Dad just said it's okay for us to get together. How about tomorrow? I'm volunteering over at

CARL—that's the animal shelter here in Willow Creek, remember?—but I'll be finished around six."

"Perfect," Cam said immediately. "How about if I pick you up there? Maybe we can grab something to eat and catch up."

"Okay. I can't wait to see you again."

"That goes triple for me," Cam replied. "I always thought you were the cutest girl in Virginia, you know. I can't wait to see how much cuter you must be now that you're all grown up."

Carole gulped. Cam had always been nice and polite, but he'd never said things like that to her before. "Okay," she said after a brief pause. "Um, I'll see you tomorrow, then."

She hung up the phone. Noticing that her father was gazing at her expectantly, she smiled weakly. "I, uh, just remembered a footnote I forgot to add to my paper. I'd better go do it while I'm thinking about it."

She raced out of the kitchen and up the stairs, wondering why the thought of seeing Cam again after all this time made her feel so nervous and flustered. She was still stunned at the comment he'd made about thinking she was cute. It wasn't the kind of thing she was used to hearing from guys, and she wasn't quite sure how to take it. Especially from Cam.

I guess people change as they grow up, she told herself as she walked into her room and shut the door. *I'm not the same person I was back when Cam knew me. And I guess he's not quite the same person I knew then, either.*

She didn't know if she liked that thought or not. But there wasn't much she could do about it, except hope that she would like the new Cam just as much as she'd liked the old one.

TWO

"Hi, Stevie. What are you up to?"

Stevie glanced up from prying a clod of dirt out of the heel of one of her good riding boots and saw Callie Forester smiling at her from the doorway of Pine Hollow's student locker room. "Hey, Callie," she said, letting the boot fall into her lap and pushing a wavy strand of dark blond hair out of her eyes. "Just puttering around, I guess. Belle's having her dinner, and Phil's picking me up here in a little while." She rolled her eyes. "Good thing, too. My darling brother disappeared with the car hours ago without bothering to let anyone know where he was going or when he'd be back. So I'm stuck with my own two feet." She snorted. "Brothers. You can't live with 'em, and you can't conk 'em on the head and toss 'em in the river. Not if anyone's watching, anyway."

Callie chuckled. "Hey, I've been there," she said. "Scott's not bad as brothers go, but he can still be a major pain sometimes."

"You're lucky you have only one, instead of three like I do." Stevie stood and tossed her boots in the general direction of her cubby. One landed inside, while the other bounced off the edge and ended up on the floor. With a loud groan, she hopped over the bench and leaned down to pick it up. She wasn't actually as annoyed with Alex as she was letting on to Callie. Normally she would have been downright irate if her twin had taken off that way with the car the two of them shared, but these days she was trying to cut him some slack. He wasn't saying much about the situation between him and Lisa, but she knew it had to be tearing him up to be separated from her, even if it was only temporary. "What about you?" she asked Callie, noticing as she straightened up again that her friend was dressed in breeches and boots. "Have you been training? I didn't even realize you were here."

"I wasn't." Callie's smile faded slightly. "Actually, I just got back from looking at a horse."

"Really?" Stevie leaned forward, interested. Now that she was finally recovered from the accident, Callie was shopping for a new competition horse so that she could get back into endurance riding in a serious way. Judging from the expression on Callie's face, however, the horse she'd just seen wasn't going to be the one. "A dud?"

"Sort of." Callie sighed and stepped farther into the room, tugging distractedly on her long, pale blond ponytail. "This one sounded so perfect on paper, too. Arabian gelding, eight years old, sound and willing. What they didn't tell me over the phone is that he's about as balanced as a car with a flat tire."

Stevie nodded. She didn't know nearly as much about endurance riding as Callie did, but she knew enough to know that balance was very important. "Is it something you could work on?"

Callie shrugged. "Probably," she said with a frown. "But it would mean serious remedial training. I would have to teach him a whole new way to move, work on getting a rounded outline, the whole nine yards. It hardly seems like a worthwhile use of my time, since I'm sure there must be plenty of horses out there that already have that training, or at least have more natural balance."

"I'm sure you're right," Stevie agreed as Max Regnery hustled into the room. He was carrying a small poster, which he hurriedly began tacking to the bulletin board across from the wall of cubbies.

Callie blew out a long, frustrated sigh. "So why do all my prospects seem to have serious flaws?"

Stevie wasn't always the most patient person in the world, but she couldn't help thinking that Callie sounded awfully pessimistic for someone who had only been seriously shopping for a horse for a few days. Before she could say so, though, Max glanced over at them.

"I know what you mean," he said to Callie

abruptly. "I'm having the same problem looking for a new stable hand."

Stevie blinked at Max in surprise. She'd known that the stable owner was looking for someone to join Pine Hollow's small full-time staff. She had also noticed that he'd seemed even gruffer and more over-worked than usual lately. But until that moment, she hadn't really connected the two facts. "Really, Max?" she asked. "That's weird. I would think that all kinds of people would be dying to work here."

"Uh-huh," Max replied grimly. "All kinds. Like a couple of college students looking for beer money who've never been inside a stable, and an eighty-two-year-old grandmother who says she loves animals and can handle anything that doesn't involve too much lifting or walking, and even one young man who ad-mitted—after I wasted ten minutes talking to him, mind you—that he's 'sort of' allergic to horses. Talk about a major flaw!" Max sighed. "Trust me, Callie, you have it easy. I'm starting to think you'd have a better chance of winning the Tevis Cup on a Shetland pony than I do of finding a decent stable worker."

Callie smiled uncertainly. "Wow," she said. "It's re-ally that bad?"

"Just about." Max sighed and ran one callused hand over his short-cropped hair. "It's just about the worst time of year to be short-staffed, too."

"Wait a second." Stevie was sympathetic to Max's

31

problems, but that last part sounded kind of odd to her. "What's the big deal about this time of year? I would think it would be easier to do without someone now than most other times."

Max glared at her. "Oh, really, Stevie?" he said sternly. "When was the last time you managed a stable?"

Stevie shrugged. "Come on, Max," she said appeasingly. "I'm just saying, it's not like it would be in spring or summer or even earlier in the fall when there are horse shows and rallies and riding camp and stuff. Even Pony Club doesn't usually meet after about the first week of December. I mean, a lot of students don't even ride at all over the holidays."

"Exactly." Max crossed his arms over his chest and stared at her evenly. "And each student that doesn't bother to ride is one more student who isn't here exercising horses, grooming them, cleaning tack, mixing grain, bringing down hay, and mucking stalls."

Stevie winced, finally getting the point. For as long as she had been riding at Pine Hollow, Max had insisted that all his riders pitch in and help with stable chores, as well as help to care for the horses they rode. It was a good way to teach important skills and responsibilities, but it was also the most effective way of keeping costs down. Stevie knew there were plenty of other riding stables in the area with larger staffs and less grunt work for the riders, but most of them charged almost double the price that Max did for lessons and boarding. "Okay, okay," she said, holding up both hands and glancing at Callie for help. "I see what you're saying. But still—"

"Still," Max interrupted, "the horses have to eat on Christmas and New Year's and Thanksgiving, just like every other day of the year. Plus it's just getting cold, which means keeping track of turnout rugs and deciding who gets clipped and when. Besides, even though Pony Club is suspended, there are still adult lessons to keep track of and boarders' schedules to deal with. And then of course . . ." Instead of continuing, Max just waved one hand at the poster he'd just hung on the bulletin board.

For the first time, Stevie glanced at it. The poster was handwritten in large block letters, which read:

ALL PERMISSION SLIPS FOR THE STARLIGHT RIDE MUST BE IN BY DEC. 22. **NO EXCEPTIONS!**

"Oh, yeah," she said. "The Starlight Ride." She couldn't help smiling at the thought of one of her all-time favorite Pine Hollow traditions. Every year on Christmas Eve, a large group of riders set out, guided by torches, for a nighttime trail ride through the woods, culminating in a festive bonfire in the Willow Creek town square, where much of the community turned out to greet the riders. The Starlight Ride was mostly for the younger students at the stable, and Stevie hadn't gone for the past several years. But she still carried fond memories of trotting through the woods by the soft, flickering light of torches;

enjoying the crisp, cool air; singing Christmas carols; and looking forward to having hot chocolate and cookies in front of the roaring bonfire.

"The Starlight Ride," Max repeated. He didn't sound nearly as pleased at the idea. "Yes, it's a nice tradition, but it's a lot of work, too."

Stevie cocked a eyebrow at him skeptically. "Well, sure," she said as diplomatically as she could. She could tell Max was in a testy mood, and she didn't want to antagonize. "I guess that's true. It's never easy to control and coordinate a bunch of intermediate and beginning riders on a nighttime trail ride."

"That's not all there is to it, Stevie," Max snapped.

Stevie winced. *So much for being tactful,* she thought ruefully.

Max wasn't finished. He was already ticking things off on his fingers. "First, I have to plan ahead to get permits from the township for the bonfire, as well as providing them with proof of insurance so we'll be allowed to ride within the town limits. Then I have to run off copies of the permission slip for all my students, along with plenty of extras, since about half the students manage to lose theirs before they even get it home." He frowned and continued. "Then there's dragging down all the torches from the storage loft and checking to make sure they're all in working order. Collecting permission slips—that's always a fun one. And then there's the details of the ride itself to worry about: checking the tack, making sure the trails are all clear, setting out the torches to mark the trail and assigning volunteers to keep an eye on them so there's no risk of fire, convincing yet more volunteers to make the refreshments and bring them over to the bonfire. And, of course, I have to arrange for someone to drive the truck over to town, not to mention loading it up with hay first. And then unloading the leftovers afterward."

For once, Stevie was at a loss for words. *Wow*, she thought. *I guess I never thought about all that stuff. It really does sound like a big job.*

"Seems like a big hassle," Callie commented.

Max shrugged. "It *is* a hassle," he said bluntly. "Sometimes I'm not sure it's really all worth it."

Stevie gasped. This time she knew exactly what to say. "Don't say that, Max," she protested quickly. "It *is* worth it. The Starlight Ride is a wonderful thing, and I'm just sorry I took it so much for granted before. We all did, I guess. But I want to make up for that now—I'll help you out this year. As much as you need me to."

"Really?" Max shot her a sharp, thoughtful glance. "Well, I can't say no to that, Stevie. If you really want to help out, I'd be happy to have you."

"I really want to," Stevie assured him eagerly. Even though she'd only had the idea fifteen seconds before, she was already getting excited about it. She could tell that Max was at his wits' end—he had to be, if he was questioning the Starlight Ride. "It'll be fun."

"Well, I can't promise you that," Max muttered, glancing at his watch. "But thanks. I'll talk to you more about this later, all right? I can't stand around here chatting all day. Red and Denise are both off today—some kind of anniversary, how could I say no to that?—and there are a million and one things to do around here as usual." He hardly bothered to finish the sentence before turning on his heel and striding out of the room without a backward glance.

Stevie stared after him, letting out a low whistle. "Whew!" she commented. "Max sure is cranky today, isn't he?"

Callie glanced at the door, looking distracted. "I guess."

Stevie couldn't help being a little surprised, not only at her friend's apparent disinterest in Max's sudden attack of the grumpies, but also at the fact that Callie hadn't spoken up and volunteered her help for the Starlight Ride as well. *If Lisa or Carole had been here, they would have offered to help in a heartbeat,* Stevie thought.

Then she realized that she was being a little unfair. Callie had only lived in Willow Creek for about six months. This would be her first Christmas at Pine Hollow.

Of course, Stevie thought, a little relieved. *She probably never even heard of the Starlight Ride until five minutes ago. She has no idea how special it really is.*

"Hey, Callie," she said. "You're probably wondering exactly what this Starlight Ride business is all about, huh?"

"What?" Callie blinked at her. "Oh. Um, isn't it, like, a Christmassy sort of trail ride for the younger kids?"

"Well, sure," Stevie said brightly. "But it's more than that. It's one of Pine Hollow's totally cherished traditions. See, everyone goes on this cool trail ride on Christmas Eve. For a lot of the younger riders, it's the first time they've ever been out on the trails after sunset. Oh! And by the way, it also explains where Starlight got his name. See, back when we were all in junior high, Carole was, like, *dying* for her own horse. So her dad decided to buy her one, and he even managed to trick her into taking a test ride on the one he was thinking about getting. . . ." Seeing that Callie's blue eyes seemed to be glazing over, Stevie hurried on. "Well, that's sort of a long story. Anyway, the important part is, he managed to find the perfect horse: Starlight. Only he was called Pretty Boy then." She wrinkled her nose. "Can you imagine? Talk about a lame name! But anyhow, the night of the Starlight Ride, Carole actually ended up riding him, and she didn't even know he was hers. Not until afterward, I mean—that's when the colonel told her. And—"

"Hi, you two," Scott Forester said at that moment, stepping into the room.

Stevie gulped. "Scott," she blurted out, forgetting

all about her story. "Uh, hi. What are you doing here?"

Scott shrugged. "Waiting for Callie, of course," he replied. He grinned. "You have a problem with that, Lake?"

Stevie laughed nervously. "Oh! No, of course not," she said hastily. "I'm here waiting for Phil myself. We have a date. You know, um, a date."

"That's nice." Scott leaned against the wall just inside the doorway. "Almost ready to go, Callie?"

"Almost," Callie replied, hurrying toward her cubby. "Just let me dig out my spare breeches. I think they're in here somewhere."

As Callie began shuffling through the stuff in her cubby, Stevie smiled awkwardly at Scott. Now that she knew how he felt about her, it was getting harder and harder to act normal around him. *I wish this would just go away,* she thought desperately. *Scott knows how tight Phil and I are. So why'd he have to go and complicate things by getting this huge crush on me? I guess it's what I get for being so irresistible. . . .*

"What's going on, Stevie?" Scott asked, interrupting her thoughts.

"Huh?" Stevie gulped, wondering if he'd somehow read her mind. "Uh, what do you mean?"

Scott shrugged and crossed his arms over his chest, gazing at her critically. "You have a weird look on your face, and you're staring at me like I just grew an extra nose. So spill it. What's up?"

"Nothing!" Stevie blurted out, willing herself not to blush. Even Callie was glancing over her shoulder curiously. "Er, I was just, that is, um—"

"Evening, boys and girls!" Phil Marsten's voice rang out cheerfully as he walked into the room. "What's going on?"

"Hi!" Stevie exclaimed, relieved at the interruption. She raced over to meet her boyfriend with a big hug and kiss. "You're here!"

Phil looked a little surprised at the enthusiasm of her greeting, though he didn't complain. "Right on schedule," he agreed, tucking a strand of hair behind Stevie's ear as she clung to him. He glanced at Callie and Scott. "Hey there, Foresters," he added.

"So where are you and the little woman off to this evening?" Scott asked Phil, stepping over and clapping him on the shoulder.

"Oh, we're not sure yet," Stevie put in hastily, not wanting Phil to tell him that the two of them had talked about going bowling that night. Even though she loved bowling, it didn't sound very romantic, and Stevie didn't want Scott to get the idea that she and Phil were losing the magic. "Probably someplace totally romantic," she added brightly. "You know what a romantic guy Phil is." She still had one arm around Phil's waist, and she squeezed him tightly.

Phil shot her a strange look, but he didn't contradict her. "So how's the horse hunt going, Callie?" he asked instead. "Find the next Tevis Cup champ yet?"

Callie snorted in reply. "Not even close," she replied shortly.

"We've been looking," Scott said easily, obviously trying to make up for Callie's rather rude response. "But Callie hasn't seen anything too promising so far."

"Bummer," Phil replied, lifting his arm from Stevie's waist and resting it casually on her shoulder. "But I'm sure the right horse will come along soon and it'll all be worth the wait."

Callie didn't respond. She was staring into her cubby so intently that Stevie wasn't sure she'd even heard Phil's comment. Deciding it was time for a change of subject, she glanced up at her boyfriend. "So did you hang out with A.J. this afternoon?"

Phil nodded. "We went for a ride, then watched the game over at my house."

"How is he these days?" Scott asked, his carefree expression shifting into one of concern. "Has he started dealing with the adoption thing yet?"

Stevie thought that was a good question, and not an easy one to answer. A couple of months earlier, A.J. had accidentally discovered that he had been adopted as a baby. The parents who had raised him had never breathed a word about it in sixteen years, and A.J. had taken the news pretty hard. Overnight, he had changed from the high-spirited, funny, likable guy Stevie had always known into an unpredictable stranger, with moods that ranged from frighteningly manic to downright sullen. He'd also seemed on the verge of developing a serious drinking problem, though fortunately his friends had managed to convince him that that wasn't the way to deal with his pain.

"He's doing okay, I think," Phil replied. "He's even started talking about tracking down his birth parents."

"Really?" Stevie was surprised. The last she'd heard, A.J. was still having trouble discussing the whole topic of his adoption, even with his best friend. "He really said that?"

"Well, he sort of hinted," Phil replied. "I can tell he's got mixed feelings about the whole deal. And he's nervous, of course."

"Sure," Scott said with a nod. "Anyone would be."

Phil nodded and gently extricated himself from Stevie's grasp. "I tried to convince him to talk to his folks about it," he said, stepping over to the bench in front of the cubbies and propping one foot on it so that he could reach the laces of his basketball shoe, which had come untied. "Even though it was a closed adoption—you know, as in the whole deal was a big secret, and the McDonnells never even knew the birth mother's name—they may have some idea how to start looking. And I'm sure they'd be supportive."

Stevie wasn't quite so convinced of that. She liked A.J.'s parents, and she knew they meant well, but they weren't the most open or demonstrative people in the world. She wondered just how they were going to deal with the idea that their son wanted to uncover his roots. "Poor A.J.," she said, pushing those thoughts aside. "Did you try to talk him into coming to the CARL thing on Friday? It might cheer him up a little to get out and have some fun with us."

"The what?" Scott asked, wrinkling his forehead in confusion. "Who's Carl?"

Stevie winced, realizing too late that Scott had no idea what she was talking about. "It's not a who, it's a what," she explained reluctantly. As soon as Scott found out about the fund-raiser, he would probably decide to go as a way to spend more time with her. Stevie stepped over to Phil, resting one hand on the back of his neck just to reinforce the fact that they were a couple. "*CARL* stands for 'County Animal Rescue League'—it's the shelter in town. They're having a fund-raising party on Friday night."

"Really?" Scott looked interested. "Sounds like a good cause. Who all is going?"

"Oh, um, just a few people," Stevie replied. "Phil and I are going together, of course. And Lisa and Carole will be there."

"I can't believe Stevie didn't tell you about it before this," Phil commented, swatting Stevie's hand away from his neck. "Quit it, that tickles." He straightened up and stretched. "Anyway, you two should definitely come. The tickets are a little steep, but like you said, it's a good cause. And it should be fun. This is the first year Stevie and I are going, but there's supposed to be a good band for dancing, and a bunch of restaurants donate food, and there will be door prizes and stuff."

Stevie held her breath, waiting for Scott to suggest that they all go together. Instead he nodded thoughtfully. "Sounds interesting."

Stevie was relieved. *Maybe he's starting to catch on,* she thought. *No matter how much he wants me, he must realize there's no way. Right?*

Not wanting to take any chances, she grabbed Phil's hand. "Come on," she said. "Let's go before Max comes along and makes us do stable chores."

Soon the two of them were stepping through the large front doors of the stable into the clear December evening. The sun had just set and there was a serious chill in the air, but Stevie could hear riders still practicing in the main schooling ring nearby. When she glanced over, she saw a couple of students trotting side by side across the ring. Squinting in the fading light, she saw that one of the horses was Starlight. Rachel Hart, a seventh-grader, was in the saddle.

"Okay," Phil said bluntly. "What was that all about?"

"What was what all about?" Stevie asked innocently, keeping her gaze on the horses in the ring. Rachel was pulling ahead of the other rider, a girl named Juliet who was aboard her quarter horse

43

gelding, Pinky. Stevie couldn't help admiring Rachel's form as she posted cleanly.

She rides almost as well as Carole did at that age, she thought. *Pretty impressive. No wonder Carole asked her to help her take care of Starlight while she's grounded.*

Phil squeezed her hand, which he was still holding as they walked. "Yo," he said. "You know what I'm talking about. You were acting like a total freak back there with Scott and Callie. What's up?"

Stevie finally met his eye. "Oh," she said meekly. "Um, yeah. I guess I had a few things on my mind."

"Such as?" Phil asked expectantly.

Stevie hesitated as they wandered toward the parking lot on the far side of the stable yard. So far she hadn't told anyone except Carole and Lisa about her suspicions about Scott. *Should I tell Phil?* she wondered uncertainly. *I don't want to mess up his friendship with Scott or anything.*

Still, she knew she couldn't keep her thoughts from him much longer. The two of them had always been honest with each other, and she didn't want to start keeping secrets now. She would just have to trust her boyfriend to be mature enough to handle the news without going ballistic.

"Okay," she said, taking a deep breath and pulling him forward until they were standing beside his father's car, a black sedan. Stevie turned to face him, taking his other hand in hers and looking him square in the face. "Here it is. But you have to promise not to get mad."

"What is it?" Phil looked worried. "Spill it, Stevie."

Stevie took another deep breath. "It's about Scott. I think he likes me."

Confusion shadowed Phil's expression. "Huh?" he said. "Of course he does. I thought you guys dealt with this ages ago. Why? Has he been talking about the accident again?"

"No, no!" Stevie dropped his hands and waved her own, realizing he'd totally misunderstood what she was trying to say. "That's not what I'm talking about. I mean I think he *likes* me. As in, wants me, needs me, totally digs me."

Phil blinked. "Huh?"

"I know," Stevie said. "I was pretty shocked, too. I mean, he knows perfectly well that you and I are— What?" she interrupted herself, noticing that Phil was smiling. "I'm not kidding. He keeps talking to me at school all the time, and he's been hanging around the stable . . ."

"Oh, really?" Phil said, his grin breaking into a chuckle. A moment later he started to laugh. "Talking to you at school, huh?" he chortled. Then he laughed so hard that he bent over, resting both hands on his knees as his whole body shook

45

uncontrollably. "S-Stevie and S-S-Scott, sittin' in a tree!" he gasped out after a moment, leaning back against his car for support.

"Hey! What's so funny?" Stevie said irritably, poking him hard in the shoulder. "Didn't you hear what I just said? Another guy likes me. A good-looking guy. Smart, too. So what's the big joke?"

"Sorry," Phil gasped, wiping his eyes with the backs of his hands. "Um, it's just that, well, don't take this the wrong way. But are you really sure about this? Because I have to tell you, I just don't see it."

Stevie was annoyed. Crossing her arms over her chest, she glared at him. "Why not?" she demanded. "Is it so hard to believe that a cool guy like Scott would be interested in me?"

"Of course not," Phil said apologetically, though the effect was spoiled by the snicker that escaped. He reached for her and pulled her to him. "Any guy in the world would be crazy not to want you."

Stevie kept herself stiff for a couple of seconds before relaxing into his embrace. "Okay," she mumbled into his shoulder. "So then what's the big joke?"

"Oh, I don't know." Phil rubbed her back. "I guess it was just what you said about him talking to you at school. I mean, have you ever met a person Scott *didn't* want to talk to?"

"Okay, okay," Stevie replied, pulling away and looking Phil in the eye again. "But I really think there's more to this than just, you know, plain old friendliness. It's just a vibe I get when he's around. Like he's fishing for something."

"Hmmm." Phil was still smiling. "That's interesting. Tell me, do you get the same vibe from anyone else? Because, you know, I caught Max looking at you the other day after you dropped that bucket full of water on the floor. Maybe that means *he* secretly wants you, too."

Stevie frowned. "Very funny," she mumbled, kicking at the gravel of the parking lot.

"And then there's good old Starlight." Phil was gazing across the stable yard in the direction of the schooling ring, an expression of mock concern on his face. "Don't think I haven't noticed the way he's always nosing at you when you walk by his stall."

Stevie rolled her eyes. *Oh well,* she thought resignedly. *I suppose I should be glad that Phil isn't the jealous type. Still, it would be nice if he were at least a tiny bit upset at the idea that there might be some competition out there.*

She couldn't really get too worked up about that idea, though. She'd seen what jealousy and suspicion had done to Lisa and Alex's relationship, and it wasn't pretty. "Okay, whatever," she told Phil, forcing a smile. "It's just a theory. It's not like I'm planning to say anything to him. I'm sure he'll get over it if I just ignore it, right?"

"Definitely," Phil agreed. "I don't know about Starlight, though. I think he's had this crush on you for years."

Stevie couldn't help laughing. "Yeah, well, you'd better watch yourself," she teased in return. "I've always thought Starlight was pretty handsome. If you don't behave . . ." She waggled one finger in front of his face.

Phil grabbed it with a grin and pulled her a little closer. "Is that a threat?" he murmured, his breath warm on her face.

"No. But this is." Stevie snuggled into his arms. "If you breathe a word of this to anyone—the Scott stuff, I mean—I'll kill you. And then Starlight will have me all to himself."

Lisa lowered her book with a sigh and sat up straighter on her bed, rubbing her eyes. She'd just read the same paragraph about six times and still had no idea what it said. Her mind kept drifting. She couldn't help wondering what Alex was doing at that moment. Was he at home, missing her like she was missing him? Or was he out somewhere having fun, not thinking about her at all? She wasn't sure which scenario made her heart ache more.

So this is what it's like being single again, she thought, tossing the book onto her nightstand and swinging her legs over the edge of the bed. *This is what it's like to be a social loser, spending Saturday*

*night with no plans at all. This is what it's like to be
without Alex in my life.*

She knew she was being melodramatic, but she
didn't care. It was only a little after eight o'clock, and
it already felt as if the evening had dragged on forever. Deciding that she couldn't go one more minute
without human company, Lisa stood up and headed
for the door.

Her mother was sitting in her usual spot on the living-room couch, watching some old black-and-white
movie on TV. She had spent a lot of time doing that
lately, ever since her first postdivorce boyfriend had
dumped her the weekend after Thanksgiving. "Hello,
dear." Mrs. Atwood glanced up as Lisa entered the
room, giving her a smile that looked so forced it was almost painful to see. "Heading out with your friends?"

Lisa grimaced, glancing down at her plaid flannel
pajama top, frayed sweatpants, and fuzzy blue slip-
pers. "Dressed like this?" she said. "No, I don't think
so. Besides, my friends all have other plans tonight."

"Of course," Mrs. Atwood said with a frown.
"That's the trouble with friends. They always desert
you when you need them the most."

Even in her current melancholy mood, Lisa wasn't
about to agree with that. "No, it's not like that,
Mom," she said, sinking down onto the arm of an
upholstered chair. "If I really needed them they'd be
here in a second."

Mrs. Atwood shrugged, her gaze straying back to

49

the television. "If you say so," she said, sounding doubtful. "But the longer I live, the more I come to realize that people usually find a way to let you down in the end. No matter how much you think you can count on them."

Lisa opened her mouth to argue, then shut it again. Sure, her mother was being pretty negative. And Lisa really believed that her mother's bad attitude had more to do with her miserable life than the divorce or anything else. But was Lisa all that much better off herself when you got right down to it?

I'm sitting here on Saturday night, dressed like a slob, talking to my mother, she thought. *My friends are all out having a good time. I've got no boyfriend. My parents both think I screwed up my life by picking the college of my choice without their help.* She did her best to banish that last thought. In her current state of mind, she didn't want to start brooding over that whole situation. She had responded to her acceptance to Northern Virginia University without telling anyone, and her parents couldn't seem to let it go, even though Lisa was still convinced that NVU was the best school for her. *It's all a mess. Even my favorite horse is dead. What's left for me?*

But the question had hardly even formed in her mind before Lisa knew the answer. Her friends. No matter what, she still had her friends.

I guess that's the big difference between Mom and me, she thought, feeling a sudden pang of pity for her mother, sharp and deep. *I know there are plenty of people who care about me and want me to be happy—Stevie and Carole and their families, Max and the others at Pine Hollow. But who does Mom have? She doesn't really have any close friends around here. Just about the only person she talks to besides me is Aunt Marianne. And I know she doesn't even talk to her as often as she wants to because she lives in New Jersey.*

Mrs. Atwood was staring at the TV with a slight frown on her lined face. "Yes, most people let you down in the end," she muttered, reaching for the glass of white wine on the coffee table. She seemed to be talking more to herself than to Lisa. "It just makes you realize how completely empty your life really is."

"Um, I'd better go back up and do some homework," Lisa mumbled, knowing that if she hung around her mother much longer she was liable to end up in tears. And that was just about the only thing that would make her feel like even more of a loser than she already did.

Fleeing back to her room, Lisa flopped onto her bed and hugged her pillow to her chest, glancing at the clock. Eight-thirteen. Yes, maybe she was in better shape than her mother. But just at the moment, that wasn't a whole lot of comfort.

"Bye," Stevie said, leaning over to give Phil one last kiss as she reached for the door handle. "Maybe I'll see you tomorrow."

51

"Hold it." Phil switched off the ignition. "Is that any way to say good night to the guy who bought you a pineapple-and-pistachio sundae—and then had to sit there and watch you eat it?" He grinned and looped his arm around her, pulling her close. "It's payback time, baby."

Stevie giggled. "Well, okay. I guess you earned it," she joked. Doing her best to wrap her arms around him without getting them tangled in his seat belt, she tilted her face up to receive his kiss. For a moment she forgot about everything and everyone else. Then an image of her parents floated into her mind, and reluctantly she pulled away. "I'd better go in," she said. "It's getting close to curfew, and even though I'm technically on the property already, I don't want to take any chances arguing that with a couple of lawyers like Mom and Dad."

Phil chuckled. "Okay." He planted one last kiss on the tip of her nose. "See ya."

As she walked toward the front door, humming cheerfully under her breath, Stevie glanced toward the garage. Both her parents' cars were parked inside, but there was no sign in the driveway of the rattletrap blue two-door she and Alex shared.

Stevie stopped humming and frowned. Glancing at her watch, she saw that it was almost midnight, their weekend curfew. "Where is he?" she muttered with a flash of worry. Alex had to be awfully upset, even if he wasn't showing it much—after all, this was his first weekend apart from Lisa. Stevie hated to think that he might do something stupid because of that, like miss curfew and get himself grounded.

Before she could figure out what to do, she heard the sound of a motor heading down the street. Hurrying a little farther down the driveway, she squinted against the brightness of the headlights, trying to see the car behind the lights. A second later she jumped back onto the lawn as the car spun around the corner and coasted to a stop.

Whew, Stevie thought with relief. *In just under the wire.*

She waited until Alex had climbed out and was turning to close the car door before clearing her throat loudly. Alex jumped about a foot in the air and spun around. "Stevie!" he gasped, grabbing his chest. "You almost gave me a heart attack! What are you doing standing around out here in the middle of the night?"

"Never mind that," Stevie snapped, her hands on her hips. "Where were *you*? I was about to call out the National Guard."

For a moment Alex didn't answer. He swung the car door shut, giving it an extra nudge with his foot to make sure the sometimes sticky latch was fast. Then he turned and smiled at Stevie. "Don't worry, Mom," he teased. "I made curfew, didn't I?"

Stevie scowled at him. "Very funny. So where were you all this time? By the way, don't think I didn't notice that you took off with the car without bothering to let me know."

"Sorry about that." Alex didn't sound particularly apologetic. "But I needed it. I, um, had a date."

Stevie's jaw dropped. "A date?" she repeated. "What are you talking about?"

Alex shrugged, not quite meeting her eye. "Hey, that was the deal, remember?" he said. "Lisa wanted us to see other people. So I asked someone out."

"Who?" Stevie asked, still trying to take in what her brother was saying. Alex had gone out on a date already—just two days after he and Lisa had agreed to take a break from their relationship? It was too bizarre.

"None of your business." Alex was starting to look annoyed.

"Who?" Stevie said again, more firmly this time. "You might as well tell me now, because you know I'll get it out of you sooner or later."

Alex rolled his eyes. "Whatever," he muttered. "It was Nicole, okay?"

"Nicole Adams?" Stevie really couldn't believe her ears now. "You're kidding! You didn't really ask out a loser bimbo like her, did you?"

"Shut up, Stevie." Alex frowned and brushed past her, heading for the house. "I can see whoever I want, and I don't care what you think about it."

Stevie just stood there and watched him go, her

mind struggling to catch up with this new information. *Nicole Adams?* she thought in disbelief. *Is he serious?*

Nicole was a junior at Fenton Hall, and Stevie had known her for years. She was part of a group of shallow, silly, snobby girls at school led by Veronica diAngelo, one of Stevie's least favorite people. Until a couple of months ago Stevie would have said that she and Nicole had absolutely nothing in common. But that had changed—sort of. Nicole had suddenly turned up at Pine Hollow one day, announcing that she was going to start taking riding lessons.

But it actually began before that, Stevie reminded herself reluctantly. *At that party we threw, Alex and Nicole were drooling all over each other on the dance floor. . . .*

She shuddered at the image. At the time, she had excused her brother's behavior by reminding herself that he was drunk. But since then, she'd noticed Alex and Nicole hanging out together more than once, at the stable as well as at school.

Still thinking about that, she headed inside, where Alex was hanging up his coat in the front closet. For a moment Stevie was tempted to grab him and shake him and demand what on earth he was thinking. How could he go from a great girl like Lisa to a total loser like Nicole?

But she controlled herself. "Well, good night," she said as calmly as she could. "See you in the morning."

Alex looked surprised but relieved. "Good night, Stevie."

After all, it won't do any good to make a bigger deal out of this than it deserves, Stevie thought as she climbed the stairs toward her room. *So I'll just have to sit back, bite my tongue, and wait for it to pass.*

THREE

"I'll be out in a sec," Callie told Scott the next morning, unhooking her seat belt as her brother pulled into Pine Hollow's parking area with a spray of gravel. "You don't have to come in."

"No hurry. I'll just stretch my legs for a minute," Scott said, turning off the ignition. "Besides, I think I may have left my chem notebook here on Friday. I'd better look for it."

Callie shrugged. "Okay, but don't wander off. My appointment is for eleven-thirty, and I don't want to be late." Without waiting for her brother's reply, she hurried toward the stable. She was feeling anxious and disgruntled—she hated to be late, and she hated it even more when it was her fault.

Why couldn't I keep track of a simple piece of paper? she thought irritably as she strode across the entryway. *I mean, I took the trouble to write down the address. The least I could do was not lose it for a whole three days.*

She shook her head, disgusted with herself. She'd

taken down the information carefully, and she wasn't usually so scatterbrained. She knew she'd had the paper on Friday in chemistry class, because she'd pulled it out to double-check the time. But somehow it must not have made it back into her bag after that, though she hadn't noticed it was missing until just an hour earlier when she was getting ready to go. She'd tried to call Pine Hollow to ask someone there to look up the address for her in the office address file, but the stable's phone had been busy for a good ten minutes, and she hadn't wanted to waste any more time. When Scott had suggested that they stop off at Pine Hollow on their way to the appointment, she had been quick to agree.

I guess I'm just kind of worked up about this horse thing, she told herself as she crossed the entryway at a brisk walk. That was true enough. In fact, she couldn't seem to think about anything else for very long these days. For a long time, most of her focus had been on getting well—recovering from the accident, learning to walk again, keeping her muscles in shape with her therapeutic riding. But now that she was officially better, she couldn't wait to get back to where she'd been before the accident, and beyond. She'd already started working on her own conditioning by training with Barq, one of Pine Hollow's horses. But Barq could only take her so far. As long as she didn't have a real endurance horse, every second that ticked by felt wasted. *I need to find the right horse,* she thought. *I can't afford to mess up here. My whole competitive career depends on that. Everything is at stake.*

When she reached the stable office, she was surprised to see that the door was closed. Callie couldn't recall the last time that had been the case—normally it was propped wide open with a bucket or the phone book or a heavy piece of tack.

"Hey," Callie called to an intermediate rider who happened to emerge from the tack room at that moment. She struggled to remember the younger girl's name. Mary? Maddie? Meg? "Um, hi," she said, giving up on the name. "Do you know if Max is in there?" She gestured to the office door.

The girl nodded. "He's interviewing someone," she said, hoisting the bridle she was carrying a little higher on one shoulder. "You know, for the stable hand job."

"Oh. Thanks." Callie glanced at the door again, sighing in frustration. She hardly noticed when the younger girl moved on.

Just my luck, she thought, checking her watch. It was already almost eleven o'clock. If she didn't get the information she needed soon, she was definitely going to be late for her appointment.

Still, she wasn't quite desperate enough to burst in on Max's interview. Not yet, anyway. Glancing at her watch again, she turned and wandered slowly down the hall, trying to keep her impatience under control.

She was nearing the end of the hall when someone came hurrying around the corner, almost crashing into her.

"Oh!" exclaimed the pudgy, moon-faced guy breathlessly, his round gray eyes wide. "Sorry, Callie."

"That's okay, George." Callie bit back a groan. It just wasn't her day. George Wheeler was about the last person she wanted to have to deal with that day.

Of course, he's the last person I want to see pretty much any day, she thought ruefully, forcing a bland smile onto her face. George was in her class at school, and he'd had a serious crush on her for a couple of months now. Callie wasn't interested in George romantically, and for a while she had been trying to convince herself that the two of them could be friends. He was smart and kind and one of the best riders at Pine Hollow, despite his decidedly unathletic appearance. But no matter how many times she'd reminded George that all she wanted was friendship, he still couldn't quite seem to get it, and his lovesick puppy-dog act was making her uncomfortable. Finally she'd decided that something had to change, so just a couple of days earlier she'd told him that she was going to have to take a break from their friendship for a while. She was hoping that would give him a chance to think about what being friends really meant. If that didn't work, she was going to have to figure out how to tell him that they couldn't be friends at all.

Thinking about that, Callie nodded to George. "Hello," she said politely, preparing to continue on past him.

But George was blocking most of the narrow hallway, and he didn't seem inclined to move out of her way. He was gazing at her with a delighted smile stretching from one pink cheek to the other, looking like a kid on Christmas morning. "What are you up to this morning, Callie?" he asked cheerfully. "Going for a ride?"

Callie blinked, wondering if he could have forgotten their agreement already. *No way,* she told herself uncertainly. *I made myself pretty clear. How could there be any mistake?*

Still, judging by the way George was standing there grinning at her, he didn't seem to remember their conversation at all. Callie cleared her throat, not quite sure what to do. Normally she didn't have trouble handling people who were causing her problems. She'd always found that the direct approach worked just fine. But George was different. Somehow he managed to keep her just off balance enough to confuse her and make her wonder if she was somehow not getting her message across as well as she thought she was.

"Um . . . ," she began, with no idea what she was going to say next. Fortunately, she happened to glance over George's shoulder and spot Stevie walking across the entryway. "Stevie!" she blurted out in relief.

Stevie looked over. Callie could almost see the wheels turning in her friend's head as she took in the situation. A moment later, Stevie was hurrying toward her and George. "Callie!" she exclaimed cheerfully, pushing her way past George. "Excuse me," she told him with an innocent smile. "I was just looking for Callie. I need to show her something. Come on, girl, this way." She grabbed Callie's hand and dragged her down the hall, past the tack room and the still-closed office door and straight into the ladies' room.

Inside, Callie collapsed limply against the chipped ceramic sink. "Whew!" she exclaimed. "Thanks, Stevie. I owe you one."

Stevie grinned. "You looked pretty desperate out there," she said frankly. "So what's going on? Don't tell me George was proposing or something. Or was he just professing his undying love again by staring at you with that goofy look he gets—sort of the same one Belle gets when she sees me coming in with a handful of carrots?"

Callie smiled weakly. She didn't particularly feel like talking about it. "Something like that," she said. "So what's new with you? Have you come up with any more brilliant ideas for the newspaper?"

"No," Stevie replied with a slight frown. "But believe me, I'm thinking." She turned and leaned against one of the other sinks, staring at herself in the ancient, slightly cloudy mirror. "It just kills me that I don't get to cover the CARL fund-raiser. Oh!" She glanced over at Callie. "You're going, aren't you?"

Callie hadn't actually thought much about it one way or the other. She had only vague memories of what the others had been discussing about CARL and the fund-raiser, but from what she did remember, it sounded like a good cause—one her parents would be happy to subsidize. "Sure," she said with a shrug. "I guess. It's not the kind of thing where I have to have a date, is it? Otherwise I guess I'm going to be stuck just going with Scott."

She was only kidding, but a genuine expression of surprise and horror crossed Stevie's face. "Oh," Stevie said.

"Just joking," Callie said, surprised at the reaction. "You have brothers—you know how it is. I'd rather go to a dance or whatever with the creature from the black lagoon than get stuck with Scott as my date."

"I know," Stevie said quickly. "Um, I was just thinking about something else."

Something about Stevie's expression made Callie think that there was more to this than she was admitting. "What?" she asked, a little worried. "Is it something to do with Scott?"

"Well . . ." Stevie paused, looking undecided. "I guess I might as well tell you. But you have to swear on your future horse's life that you won't breathe a word to anyone, okay?"

Callie couldn't help being curious now. "What is it?"

Stevie took a deep breath. "It is about Scott," she said somberly. "I think he likes me."

"Of course he does," Callie began with a shrug. "You know he thinks you're—oh!" She broke off, suddenly realizing what Stevie was trying to say. "Really?" she said doubtfully. "What makes you think that?"

"A lot of things." Stevie shoved her hands in the pockets of her jeans and leaned back against the sink. "Starting with the way he always seems to be at Pine Hollow lately, even though he doesn't really ride."

"Oh, I'm sure that's just . . ." Callie let her voice trail off, thinking a little harder about what Stevie had just said. "Now that you mention it, I'd sort of noticed that he was here a lot, too," she said. "I mean, it made sense before, when I was still on crutches and needed to come every day for therapeutic riding. It wasn't like I could walk home myself then."

"But you could now," Stevie said with a knowing nod. "So why is big brother still playing chauffeur?"

Callie shrugged, still not convinced that Stevie's theory was right. She knew that Stevie wasn't particularly sensitive, but she still didn't want to scoff outright and hurt her feelings. *After all, it's not like it's impossible that Scott could ever have the hots for someone like her,* she thought, casting a quick, appraising glance at Stevie. Even with her thick dark

64

blond hair pulled back in a messy, lopsided pony-tail and her nice figure hidden in the folds of an enormous, shapeless wool sweater, Stevie still looked good. *Maybe she's not quite as—um—well groomed as most of Scott's love interests, but it's not an impossible thing at all. In fact, considering Scott's history, the only surprising thing is that he hasn't latched on to Stevie—or any of the other girls he hangs out with—before this.*

"What?" Stevie demanded, leaning a little closer and staring Callie in the face. "What's that weird expression about? I'm right, aren't I?"

"I don't know," Callie said hastily, not wanting to give Stevie the wrong impression. "I have no idea. As far as I know for sure, he thinks of you as a good friend—nothing more or less."

"But?" Stevie prompted, obviously expecting more.

Callie hesitated. Now that they were on the subject, a few things were nagging at her. The constant presence at the stable, yes. But there was more, too. "Actually," she said slowly, "Scott *has* been acting kind of, um . . ."

"What?"

"I don't quite know how to describe it," Callie replied, picking at a rusty spot on the edge of the sink. "But when Scott's starting to get interested in someone new, he does sort of have this way about him. Like for instance, when he had a crush on this girl Jenna at our old school who was a really serious singer, he suddenly bought all these opera CDs and started listening to them all the time. Mom and Dad and I thought he was going insane until we realized that it was because of Jenna. He wanted to learn about opera because of her."

Stevie nodded, looking triumphant and a little sick at the same time. "I knew it," she said in a strangled voice. "Just like Alex wanted to learn to ride because of Lisa. And now, like Scott has practically moved into Pine Hollow to get close to me."

"Maybe," Callie said, still uncertain.

She thought back, trying to remember how Scott had acted the times she'd seen him and Stevie together. Usually when he liked a girl, it was pretty obvious. Again, now that Callie thought about it, she did seem to recall a certain dippy, dreamy expression creeping over her brother's face now and then lately. But had it been directed at Stevie? Callie just wasn't sure.

In any case, there was still one thing that was bothering her. "I don't know what he's up to," she said. "But I do know one thing. Scott has never, ever tried to break up anyone's relationship. He knows you and Phil have been together forever. There's no way he'd try to get in the middle of that."

"You think?" Stevie didn't sound quite as convinced as Callie felt. But before Callie could answer, the bathroom door swung open, almost whacking Stevie in the shoulder.

"Oops!" exclaimed the younger girl Callie had spoken to outside the tack room earlier. "Sorry. We didn't know anyone was in here."

"No problem, May," Stevie replied with a grin. "I didn't need that shoulder anyway. I always carry a spare."

Rachel Hart giggled. "I keep telling her to slow down," she said, glancing at her friend reproachfully. "Max yelled at her in class about that just this week."

May Grover—Callie had finally recalled her full name now that Stevie had greeted her—rolled her eyes and elbowed her friend in the ribs. Then she glanced at Callie. "Hey, by the way, if you're still looking for Max, his interview person finally left."

"Thanks!" Callie said, immediately forgetting all about her brother, Stevie's worries, and everything else except her errand. She headed toward the door, which Rachel was still holding partway open. Sticking her head out, she glanced down the hall. George was nowhere in sight. "Coast is clear," she told Stevie in relief, ignoring the younger girls' curious gazes. "I'm out of here."

"Good luck," Stevie said.

Already halfway out the door, Callie responded with a wave. With any luck, she could still make it to her appointment on time—or at least come close.

"It's okay, sweetie," Carole crooned, sticking her fingers through a cage door to scratch a large gray cat under its chin. "I know this smells kind of icky, but it will dry soon, I promise."

The cat meowed and rubbed against the cage door, gazing at Carole reproachfully. Carole smiled and turned away, reaching for the paintbrush she'd left balanced on top of a can of paint. Craig Skippack, the head of Hometown Hope, had assigned her to paint Cat Room B that day. It was the smallest of the three cat rooms at CARL, and Carole was already nearly finished putting a fresh coat of pale green paint on the long concrete wall facing the rows of cages. Unlike the dogs, the cats didn't have outdoor runs, which meant that there was really nowhere to put them during the painting. But one of the volunteer vets had assured Carole that as long as she left the doors and the three high, narrow windows open, the cats would be just fine.

"Anyway, just think how nice this will look when I'm done," Carole said brightly. Talking to the cats distracted her a little from thinking about Cam, and that made it easier to focus on what she was doing instead of obsessing over what it would be like to see him again. Or thinking about that comment he'd made about her being cute.

I don't know why I should be so nervous, anyway, she thought as she stepped over to the open can of paint to dip her brush in. *Cam is an old friend. I wouldn't be feeling this way if I were meeting my old friend*

Karenna today, would I? Or Christine Lonetree. Or Ali Lemmer, my best friend from kindergarten.

"Almost finished here," she told the closest cat, a sinuous snow white female with bright green eyes. "I just have to put a coat on this trim, and then all that's left is to wait for it to dry. By the time you finish your next catnap, the whole room will look brand-new."

"Well, I can see that some things never change. You're still talking to animals."

Carole gasped and spun around. "Cam!" she exclaimed. "You're here!" Fearing that she'd lost track of time, she checked her watch. "And you're early."

"Sorry." Cam smiled and stepped forward. "I couldn't wait to see you."

Carole blushed, feeling flustered and unprepared. She had planned to take a quick trip to the ladies' room and freshen up a little, maybe even rebraid her hair, before he arrived. Now she could only imagine how many paint spatters and streaks of dirt were decorating her face at the moment. The thought distracted her and made her blush deeper.

"Well?" Cam said expectantly, taking another step toward her. If he noticed that she was totally tongue-tied and befuddled, he was doing a good job of hiding it. "Don't I even get a hug?"

"Um, of course," Carole said, one hand straying to her cheek, where something seemed to be crusted and flaking. Trying not to think about that, she opened her arms as he bent down to hug her, a spicy smell—aftershave?—enveloping her along with his arms. After a moment they both stepped back. For the first time, Carole really looked at Cam. He had always been cute, with his mocha-colored skin and clear brown eyes fringed with dark lashes. But now that he was all grown up, all the soft, rounded corners of his face had matured into chiseled features that made him much more handsome than cute. He had always been tall, and his shoulders had finally caught up with his height, broadening just enough to give him the look of an athlete.

Wow, Carole thought, realizing that she was staring openly but unable to tear her eyes away. *A lot can change in four years!*

Fortunately Cam didn't seem to notice her gaping. "So," he said cheerfully, rubbing his hands together and glancing around Cat Room B. "This is where you're spending all your time these days."

"Uh-huh. And I really need to finish up here before we go," Carole replied apologetically.

"No problem," Cam said graciously. "I'll help."

He grabbed a spare brush before Carole could protest. Gulping as she looked at his spotless khaki pants and pale blue sweater, she smiled weakly. "Um, okay. If you're sure you want to."

"Absolutely," Cam replied gallantly, shooting her a smile that seemed to show every one of his straight, brilliant white teeth. "We can catch up here as well as anywhere, right?"

"Sure." Carole was relieved that he was being such a good sport. "Thanks."

Cam nodded. "Okay, so tell me everything you've been doing for the past few years," he commanded playfully. "I must know all about what I've been missing. Are you still riding at Pine Hollow?"

Carole immediately felt slightly more comfortable. After all, this was the topic that had brought them together. "Of course," she replied. "I ride there all the time—well, usually. Now that I'm grounded—"

"Oh, yeah," Cam broke in, shooting her a curious look. "What's that all about, anyway? You must've done something really bad to get in that much trouble." He smiled and winked at the word *bad*, though Carole wasn't exactly sure why.

She bit her lip and averted her eyes, feeling ashamed as she always did when she thought about cheating on that test. "It *was* pretty bad," she said softly, deciding there was no point in trying to avoid the topic. It was bound to come up sooner or later, and if Cam was going to be disgusted and decide he didn't want to hang out with a lousy cheater, better to learn that now. "It was also pretty stupid," she went on. "See, my grades were slipping a little, and you probably remember how strict Max is about that kind of thing. Anyone who falls below a C can't ride

71

until they bring up their average again." She shrugged. "I was pretty close to that line, and then I forgot to study for this history test."

"Oh!" Cam nodded knowingly. "So you flunked, and your Dad grounded you."

"Not exactly." Carole hesitated, wishing it was as simple as that. It could have been, if she hadn't done what she'd done next. "I *did* flunk the test—big time. My teacher was surprised and kept me after class to talk about it. I wound up telling her this whopper about how Dad was really sick, and I had been too worried to study. . . . Anyway, she bought it and offered a retest. But this all happened a few weeks before a big horse show, and I was so busy getting ready for that—well, I guess I just sort of forgot to study again."

"Yikes." Cam shook his head sympathetically.

"That's when the *really* bad, stupid part comes in," Carole hurried on before he could comment further. "When I realized I was going to flunk the retest, too, I was feeling pretty desperate. Like I said, the horse show was coming up. I couldn't let my grade slip, or I wouldn't be able to ride in it. That seemed like the most horrible thing in the world at the time, and so when the teacher left the room for a few minutes, I— I looked at my textbook." She turned toward Cam, lowering her paintbrush and looking him straight in the eye. "I cheated. And I kept it a secret for more than a month. When Dad found out, he just about hit the roof. And that's why I'm grounded."

She half expected Cam to be horrified—maybe even throw down his paintbrush and leave the room in disgust. But he just nodded pensively. "Rough," he commented. "Still, I guess everyone slips at least once in their life, right?"

Carole shot him a quick, relieved smile. He didn't sound judgmental at all. "I guess," she said. "And believe me, once was definitely enough. That's the last time I even *think* about cheating—on anything!"

"Hey, I believe you, beautiful," Cam said softly, reaching out his free hand to brush a strand of hair off her cheek. "You're one of the most honest people I've ever known."

Carole goggled, barely hearing the second part of his comment. *Beautiful?* she thought in amazement, her cheek tingling where he'd touched it. *Am I hallucinating, or did he just call me beautiful?*

She gulped, not wanting Cam to notice how his casual remark had totally blown her away. "Erp," she blurted out. "Um, I mean, how about you? How's Duffy doing these days?" She smiled as she thought about Cam's horse, a likable chestnut gelding named Duffy. Carole knew that the Nelsons had gone to quite a bit of trouble and expense to move Duffy across the country, and she wondered if they'd had any problems repeating the process coming back.

"Duffy? Oh, I don't have him anymore," Cam said. "I sold him a couple of years ago."

"What?" Carole was startled. Cam had always

been just as attached to Duffy as she was to Starlight. "Why?" Realizing that sounded pretty blunt, she quickly added, "Uh, I mean, what made you decide to sell him?"

Cam shrugged. "It was kind of hard to keep up with my riding out there in L.A.," he explained. "The closest stable to our new house was, like, fifteen miles away. And with the outrageous traffic out there, it could take up to forty minutes to get there sometimes."

Carole wasn't sure what to say to that. *So he gave up riding because of the commute?* she thought uncertainly, wondering if she was missing something. *He sold the horse he loved because getting to him was inconvenient?*

Suddenly she realized she was being as judgmental as she'd feared Cam would be about her cheating. After all, people usually had lots of reasons behind important decisions—reasons that might not be apparent to someone hearing about those decisions for the first time. She of all people should know that by now.

Didn't I come awfully close to selling my own horse not too long ago? she reminded herself, thinking of the difficult days and nights leading up to her decision to find Starlight a new home. The idea had been almost unthinkable at first, but eventually Carole had convinced herself that she had outgrown her beloved horse. If she wanted to continue to develop as a rider, she had to find a mount that could challenge her—and Starlight just didn't do that anymore. She had come very close to selling him to a girl from another part of the state. That hadn't worked out, and for now, Carole was putting the whole selling-Starlight plan on hold. But somewhere in the back of her mind, she knew she might have to face it again, at least if she wanted to continue competing in top-level horse shows. *If I told Cam that I'd almost sold Starlight just a few weeks ago, he'd probably be totally shocked.*

Cam was carefully touching up the trim around the doorway and hadn't noticed her consternation. "Anyway," he said after a moment, facing her again, "now that I'm back, I hope the two of us can go riding together sometime." He gave her another brilliant smile. "Just like old times."

"Just like old times," Carole repeated, strangely relieved. Cam hadn't totally lost interest in riding. He'd just put it on hold for a while, maybe decided it wasn't the only thing he liked to do.

I can't expect everyone to be as serious about it as I am, right? Carole thought. *Maybe once upon a time he was as horse-crazy as I am, but these days I guess he just has other interests, that's all. Like Stevie has student government and the school paper and all the other stuff she does. And like Lisa has her schoolwork and her relationship with Alex and her college plans.*

Before she could think much more about that,

Cam asked after Starlight and a few of the other horses he'd known at Pine Hollow. That brought her back to the here and now, and soon the two of them were chatting easily, catching up on each other's lives for the past four years. Carole told Cam about her job at Pine Hollow, her friends' lives, and her father's new career as a motivational speaker, which he'd begun after retiring from the Marine Corps. In turn, Cam updated Carole on his own family, as well as mentioning that he had been on the soccer, basketball, and track teams at his school in California and hoped to try out for varsity basketball at Arden High the following week.

Their conversation continued as they finished painting, cleaned up their supplies and themselves, and left the animal shelter, walking a few blocks to the closest eatery, the Magnolia Diner. As they entered the small, warm, grease-scented restaurant, Carole thought briefly of her appearance. She'd only had a minute to tidy herself up and wondered just how much green paint was still decorating her face. *Most girls would probably make a break for the ladies' room to check out the damage,* she thought, quickly rubbing her cheeks with a napkin when Cam turned away to read the specials board over the cash register. *But I don't want to waste time fooling around with my hair or putting on lip gloss. I'd rather stay here and talk to Cam. Anyway, he doesn't seem to mind the way I look.*

She was starting to remember exactly why she'd thought Cam was so special all those years ago. It wasn't just his charm and good looks. In fact, she'd been interested in him before they ever met in person—their first few conversations had taken place on-line. Of course, when she'd read his name on the computer screen, she'd assumed that he was a girl. . . .

She couldn't help smiling at the memory, and Cam turned his attention back to her just in time to notice. "What?" he asked quickly. "Penny for your thoughts."

"Oh!" Carole blushed slightly. "Um, I was just thinking about the first time we met. You know, when I thought *Cam* was a girl's name?"

Cam laughed. "Oh, right," he said. He leaned forward over the table, his dark eyes gleaming. "I hope you don't still have any doubt about whether I'm a girl or a guy. Do you?"

Carole blushed deeper, at a total loss as to what she was supposed to say to that. Fortunately the waitress bustled over to the table, saving her from answering. By the time Cam had totally charmed the waitress and they'd placed their order, Carole had regained control of herself. She quickly asked Cam how school was going so far, and with that, they returned to their easy, friendly conversation.

Carole hardly noticed when the waitress brought the sodas they'd ordered, or when she returned a few minutes later and dumped a steaming plate of french fries on the table between them. A strange feeling had overtaken her—one of being in the world and yet separate from it, trapped in a cozy little bubble that enclosed her and Cam. It was as if the other people in the restaurant, the other people in the world, had ceased to exist—or at least were much less important and interesting than the two of them. The feeling was new and a little scary, but Carole didn't want it to end. She wanted this conversation, this moment, to continue forever.

After a while, though, Cam looked at his watch. "Hey," he said gently. "Check it out. Time for you to go, right?"

Reluctantly, Carole glanced at her own watch. For a moment she blinked at it stupidly, unsure of what the numbers meant. Then she snapped out of it. She was due home in twenty minutes. "Oh," she said, a little surprised at the strength of her own disappointment. She still had so much to say to Cam—questions to ask him, things to discuss . . . "My car's right back there at CARL—if I walk fast, I could probably stay a few minutes longer."

Cam waggled his finger at her playfully. "Now, now. We can't have you missing curfew the first time we're together," he said lightly. "Your dad would track me down and court-martial me."

Giggling at the image, Carole shook her head. "I

doubt it," she said. "But he just might throw me in the brig."

Cam cocked his head to one side. "The brig?" he repeated. "Isn't that, like, a Navy thing? I thought your dad was in the Marines."

"Uh-huh. But the Marine Corps is part of the Navy—some say the best part." Carole picked up her soda, draining the last few drops out of the bottom. She knew that Cam was right. It wouldn't do her any good to be late. But that didn't make it any easier to drag herself away just when they were having such a nice time together.

Who knows when he'll want to hang out again? she thought, shooting Cam a quick, secret glance as he turned to smile at the waitress, who had just deposited the bill on their table. *Pretty soon he'll be settled back in his own school, with his own friends and homework and basketball games and everything else. What if he decides he doesn't have time for an out-of-town friend anymore? What if he meets someone who—* She gulped and cut off the thought before she could finish it. What was she doing? She had no idea what Cam was thinking. Just because he'd called her beautiful didn't mean he had any interest in picking up where they'd left off.

"Anyway, I guess you're right. I'd better get going," she said, reaching around to her back pocket to fish out a few crumpled bills.

"Ah-ah-ah!" Cam held up one hand and pulled out his wallet with the other. "This one's on me."

"Oh," Carole said blankly, not sure what to do. Should she argue? Insist on paying her own way? Desperately, she tried to remember anything Stevie and Lisa had ever mentioned on the subject of who paid for what on a date. But was this a date? What if it was just a friendly get-together? After all, Carole certainly wouldn't object if an old friend wanted to buy her a snack, would she?

By the time she'd sorted it out that much, Cam had already counted out enough money to cover the food and tip, and the waitress had whisked it away with a hurried thanks. Carole shrugged and stuffed her own money back in her pocket, deciding it was too late to do anything now except graciously accept his generosity.

"Thanks," she told Cam shyly. "Um, it was really great seeing you."

Instead of responding, Cam leaned farther across the table. "What are you doing tomorrow?" he asked. "Do you have to volunteer again?"

Carole shook her head. "Tomorrow's my day off," she replied. "The whole group's, actually. The vets are doing their weekly spay/neuter clinic at CARL tomorrow afternoon, so we really wouldn't be able get much done anyhow."

"Fantastic!" Cam looked inordinately pleased at

that. "Sit tight for a sec, okay? Then I'll walk you back to your car."

"Okay," Carole agreed, a little confused. First Cam had been anxious to shoo her on her way, and now he was telling her to stay longer? She watched as he hurried across the restaurant, disappearing into a narrow hallway beside the kitchen. The public rest rooms were back there, and Carole relaxed in her seat, assuming he would return in a minute or two.

While she waited, she drummed her fingers on the tabletop and thought about the afternoon. *I can't believe how nice Cam still is, after all these years,* she thought. Feeling her cheeks redden slightly, she added, *And how cute he is, too. A total hottie, as Stevie might say* . . . She giggled slightly, imagining her friend's hazel eyes widening and her lips puckering into a wolf whistle. Then she sobered again. If she were more like Stevie, maybe she wouldn't be sitting here wondering what Cam was thinking about her, about them. Stevie would just come right out and ask if he had a girlfriend back in California, if he had thought about her at all in the years they'd been apart . . .

Just then Cam returned, a little breathless, his eyes sparkling. "Hey!" he said, reaching out a hand to help her out of the booth. "Come on, let's get out of here."

Carole accepted his help, blushing slightly as she

took his hand. His skin felt cool and smooth, and his grip was firm but gentle as he led her around the tables. She expected him to drop her hand as they reached the door, but instead he squeezed it tighter as he reached to push the door open, stepping aside to let her go first, finally releasing her hand as she stepped through.

Blushing wildly at the unexpected display of chivalry, Carole waited until he'd joined her on the sidewalk and then glanced up at him shyly. "Thanks again," she began. "I really—"

"Wait." Cam cut her off with a smile. "Don't you even want to know what I was doing just now?"

Carole was startled, her face turning redder than ever as she pictured him heading toward the bathroom. "Uh, what?"

Cam looked a little confused. "I just went back there to use the pay phone," he prompted gently as they began walking slowly back toward CARL. "Guess who I called?"

"Oh! The phone!" Carole blurted out. Hiding her face, which was redder than a huntsman's scarlet coat, she fumbled in her jacket pocket, pretending to search for something. All she came up with was a frayed purple stable bandage and a tissue, so she dabbed busily at her nose with the latter and stared at the sidewalk while she waited for her cheeks to cool. "Um, who did you call?" she mumbled around the tissue.

"Your father." Cam glanced at her, apparently waiting for her reaction. "I wanted to ask his permission to see you again tomorrow. If you want to, that is."

Carole gasped. "You want to—I mean, you did? Uh, what did he say?"

"He said yes." Cam smiled. "After I did a little convincing, that is. He even said he'd waive your usual two-hour time limit at the stable if we wanted to go on a nice, long, leisurely trail ride together. So what do you say?"

Carole had no idea what to say. "Um, really?" she asked cautiously, hardly daring to believe what she was hearing. She wasn't sure which surprised her more: that Cam was so eager to see her again that he'd gone to so much trouble to arrange it, or that her father had actually agreed to the plan.

"Really," Cam replied. "Now, what's your answer?"

"Yes!" Carole blurted out. "Of course. That sounds like fun."

"Good." Cam smiled. "It's a date, then."

He kept talking as they continued toward CARL, chatting about the trails around Pine Hollow, but Carole hardly heard him. Her head was spinning. A date? Did he really mean that the way she thought he did? She still wasn't sure. Maybe it had just been a casual comment—the same sort of thing she might say when making plans with Stevie or Lisa. Then again . . .

Who cares if this is a date, as in a date *date, or just a date for two old friends to hang out?* she told herself. *Either way, I'm just happy I get to see Cam again.*

But as Cam took her elbow to steer her around a jagged crack in the sidewalk, Carole felt herself shiver slightly, even though her jacket was more than enough protection against the chilly afternoon air. She didn't know for sure yet what it meant to have Cam back in her life, but she couldn't wait to find out. Suddenly the next afternoon seemed an almost unbearably long way away.

FOUR

The next morning when she arrived at school, Stevie was so busy thinking about the list of possible *Sentinel* articles she'd come up with the night before that she didn't see Scott heading her way until he called her name. Snapping out of her trance, Stevie gulped and forced a pleasant, neutral expression onto her face. "Hi," she said as Scott reached her.

"Howdy," Scott replied cheerfully. "Looks like you're lost in space."

Stevie smiled weakly, wishing she'd decided to take the other staircase. "Oh. Uh, I was just thinking about my burgeoning career as a reporter," she said. "I'm on my way to a meeting with Theresa—you know, the editor. She likes to meet with new people for a few weeks one on one in addition to the regular staff meetings. She's waiting for me in the media room right now."

"I'll walk you there," Scott said easily. "I'm headed that direction myself. So how was your weekend?" He fell into step beside her.

Stevie bit her lip, wishing she knew what to do about Scott. The situation was becoming more and more worrisome the longer it went on. *Why can't he just get over me already?* she thought. *Then we could go back to being friends again, and everything would be just fine.*

Realizing that she was taking an awfully long time to answer a simple question, she quickly cleared her throat. "My weekend?" she said. "It was good. Great, actually. Phil and I went out on Saturday night, remember? We had a great time together. Like we always do. Very romantic."

She realized she was babbling, but if Scott noticed, he didn't comment on it. "That's cool," he said as they reached the stairs and started up them. "Hey, not to change the subject or anything, but I have a question for you. What's this Starlight Ride thing I keep hearing about?"

"The Starlight Ride?" Stevie gulped again. Until that very moment, she had always thought of the tradition as a fun, special time spent with good friends. But now, as she stole a peek at Scott beside her, she couldn't help thinking that it could be seen in another way. As a romantic evening, riding under the stars with that special someone . . . "Um, why do you ask?"

"Just curious," Scott replied with a shrug. "I already asked Veronica about it, but she said it was just, and I quote, 'some lame trail ride where people act like dorks and freeze their butts off.' "

Stevie grimaced. It was no surprise that Veronica wouldn't have anything complimentary to say about the Starlight Ride. Thanks to her obnoxious attitude and general disdain for stable rules, she'd been banned from the Starlight Ride more often than not over the years when she'd been a regular student at Pine Hollow.

"Don't listen to her," Stevie said, unable to bear the thought that Veronica was slandering one of her favorite memories. She had to correct Scott's impression, even if it meant encouraging him to imagine the two of them riding along together in the moonlight. "The Starlight Ride's great. It happens on Christmas Eve, usually right at dusk. Max lines a trail through the woods with lanterns, and everyone rides over to town, where there's this big bonfire and hot chocolate and stuff. People sing carols as they ride, and once it actually snowed, and Max turned up riding in a horse-drawn sleigh." She sighed nostalgically at the memory, one of her favorites in all her years of riding. "It's definitely more for the younger kids, though," she added hastily as Scott nodded with interest. "I mean, I haven't gone myself in a couple of years now—older, more experienced riders like my friends and I don't usually go along on the ride anymore. We just help out with the setup or whatever."

She decided there was no point in mentioning the fact that as far as she knew, Carole was the only one of her friends who had ever helped out much—if at all—with the Starlight Ride before that year.

"Hmmm," Scott said. "Sounds like a fun time."

"Oh, it is—for the younger kids," Stevie assured him. "As for the rest of us, well, we'll probably be really, really busy for the next few weeks getting everything ready." She sighed heavily and gave a dramatic shrug to emphasize her point. "The behind-the-scenes prep isn't going to be fun and games, you know. It'll be work—real, physical-labor type grunt work. And lots of it."

There, she thought with satisfaction as Scott turned away briefly to return a passing friend's greeting. *That should convince him that there won't be much point hanging around the stable for a while. Maybe by the time the Starlight Ride comes and goes, he'll have come to his senses and realized that we're meant to be just friends.* She stole another peek at Scott as he returned his attention to her, trying to gauge his reaction.

Instead of looking bored or disgusted, as she'd expected, he looked interested. "Wow," he said. "It sounds like you have your work cut out for you. Who's going to be doing all this backbreaking work, anyway? I thought Carole was still more or less grounded."

Probably trying to figure out if there's any chance of

catching me alone in the hayloft or something, Stevie thought in dismay.

"Oh, there'll be a bunch of us helping out," she assured him quickly. "You know, the regular Pine Hollow gang—me, Lisa, maybe Phil—" She made a quick mental note to invite Phil over to help. "The usual suspects. Of course, Max and Denise and Red and Ben do a lot of the work, too," she added generously, feeling a twinge of guilt at the way she was overplaying her role. Sure, she'd promised Max she would help, but that didn't mean the paid stable hands were going to be sitting around twiddling their thumbs.

"The whole gang, huh?" They had almost reached the media room by then, and Scott paused in the middle of the hallway, looking at her with interest. "There must be an awful lot to do. Sounds like you could use all the help you can get."

"Sure, I guess," Stevie replied distractedly, already thinking about her meeting with Theresa.

"Good. Then I hereby volunteer," Scott announced with a smile.

That got Stevie's attention back. "Huh?" she said. "Volunteer? For what?"

"For grunt duty. I want to help you guys out with the Starlight Ride." He shrugged and winked. "I'm sure you all can find something for a non-rider like me to do, right?"

Stevie's mind raced. "Oh, that's okay," she said

quickly, mentally kicking herself for not seeing this coming. "You really don't have to do that. I was just complaining before. We actually have everything under control, so you—"

Scott held up one hand to silence her. "I won't take no for an answer," he said with a gallant little half bow. "Just consider me an honorary stable hand."

Stevie smiled weakly. What could she say? *I could tell him I know why he's doing this,* she thought. *I could tell him I know how he feels about me.*

But somehow, it didn't seem like the right time or place. The hall was growing more and more crowded with students heading to homeroom, and Stevie was already a little late for her meeting. She would just have to figure out something later. Maybe Callie could give her some advice at lunch.

"Listen, I'd better get in there," Stevie said, gesturing toward the open door of the media room. "Theresa's waiting for me."

Without waiting for an answer, she escaped into the spacious double room that served as a home base for the school's newspaper, yearbook, and audio-visual clubs. The editor, a thoughtful, rather serious senior named Theresa Cruz, was sitting at one of the long tables scattered throughout the room, poring over the previous Friday's issue of the *Sentinel.*

"Hi," Stevie said, hurrying over to her. "Sorry I'm late."

"Good morning, Stevie." Theresa looked up,

blinking her large dark eyes. "It's okay. I was just reading over your article about the junior sociology project. It turned out very well."

"Thanks." Stevie beamed, knowing that the compliment was almost as valuable as a favorable comment from Max. Maybe Theresa wasn't constantly yelling about keeping her heels down and her elbows in the way Max did, but like Max, she didn't lavish praise on people who didn't deserve it. Even after just a week on the *Sentinel* staff, Stevie knew that. "I'm pretty proud of it. It was hard work meeting the deadline and everything, but definitely worth it."

Theresa nodded and folded the paper carefully, setting it aside atop a pile of books and notebooks. "Have a seat," she told Stevie, gesturing at the chair across from her. "I want to talk to you about your future at the *Sentinel*."

"Great!" Stevie yanked out the chair and perched on the edge, leaning forward with her elbows on the table. "I already have tons of ideas. I mean, I still wish I could do a story on the CARL fund-raiser this weekend, but I—"

"Wait, Stevie." Theresa smiled slightly. "I appreciate your enthusiasm. But I'm not sure we're ready for that just yet. After all, you just joined the paper."

"What?" Stevie was stunned and disappointed. True, Theresa had told her at the beginning that she would have to work her way up to being a full-fledged reporter. But then that junior-class project had come along, and Stevie had stepped forward to cover it, since all the other writers were busy with other stories. Her article had turned out well, as Theresa herself had just said. Didn't that mean she'd paid her dues?

"I understand that you're eager to do more writing," Theresa went on sympathetically. "But I do think you'd benefit from learning the ropes a little more before you go any further with your own writing."

"Oh," Stevie said glumly, sinking back in her seat. She was tempted to argue, to point out that she could learn *and* write at the same time. But one glance at Theresa's businesslike expression convinced her that it would be pointless. The other girl's mind was made up, and if Stevie ever wanted to see her name in a byline again, she would just have to suck it up and play the good little student for a while, even if it meant typing up the weekly lunch menu or proofreading other people's work. "Um, okay. What do you want me to do first?"

Theresa smiled. "Actually, I have a special assignment in mind for you, Stevie. An important job. I think you'd be really good at it."

Stevie sat up a little straighter, feeling a stab of excitement course through her. "Really?" she said. "An assignment? What is it?"

Theresa leaned back in her chair, stretching her arms in front of her. "As I'm sure you know, Fenton Hall's fiftieth anniversary is coming up next fall. The administration is already planning all sorts of festivities to celebrate the occasion."

Stevie nodded expectantly, resisting the urge to giggle. Theresa was just about the only person she knew who would actually use the word *festivities* without a trace of irony. The only person under age forty, anyway. "Yes," she said, keeping a straight face with difficulty. After all, she probably wouldn't get to hear about this mysterious assignment if she insulted the editor now. "I remember hearing something about that. Do you want me to write a sort of preview of all that? Talk to Miss Fenton about what she has planned?"

"Not exactly." Theresa pulled a piece of paper out of one of the notebooks in the stack beside her and glanced at it. "Do you know Cassidy Clark?"

"Sure," Stevie said with a shrug. "She's a senior, right? I think she was on the publicity committee for the student council last year." She pulled up a vague mental image of a tall, big-boned girl with light brown hair. "I don't know her very well, though."

"That's all right," Theresa said. "You'll be getting to know her a lot better soon. She's the section editor of the School News page, which means she's in charge of all this year's coverage of the anniversary celebration. She's going crazy trying to research her first article on the history of the school, and I'd like you to help her out."

"Oh." Stevie blinked, wondering exactly what

Theresa meant by that. "You mean she's going to talk about the illustrious past of Fenton Hall or whatever? Will I need to interview, like, former students about their glory days?" That didn't sound too bad. Stevie liked talking to people, and she was sure she could uncover some interesting stories if she put her mind to it.

But Theresa was already shaking her head. "I think Cassidy's on top of that," she said. "You'll mostly need to help out with the research. You know, dig through old yearbooks, newspapers, records at the township office, that kind of thing."

"Oh." Stevie's heart sank. "Um . . ."

"This is a very important project," Theresa continued. "Normally I would ask a more experienced reporter to do it, but after the good work you've already done in the past week, I think you can handle it."

Stevie smiled weakly as Theresa went on about all the important drudgery that needed to be done. As far as Stevie was concerned, a research assistant was a research assistant, no matter how thrilling Theresa tried to make it sound. Still, she could tell that the editor was sincere about thinking that Stevie should be honored by the assignment, so she did her best to look fascinated as she frantically searched her mind for a way out.

I can't just say no, she thought desperately, imagining herself trapped for the next few months in the school library, which always seemed a little like some kind of medieval jail cell anyway, with its low ceilings, musty smell, and constantly flickering fluorescent lights. *If I bag out on this, Theresa will think I'm not a team player. Then my chances of getting a decent story accepted anytime this year will be about as good as Alex's chances of making the honor roll. In other words, zipporama.*

She bit her lip, trying to come up with a way out. Maybe if she wowed Theresa with another story idea, the editor would reconsider. But as she scanned her mental list of the ideas she'd come up with so far, she wasn't sure that any of them would do the trick.

It needs to be something special, she thought. *Something that only I could do.*

Suddenly she remembered her conversation with Scott. "That's it!" she blurted out, breaking into Theresa's monologue about the importance of citing the correct sources. Catching herself, she grinned apologetically. "Um, sorry for interrupting, but I just remembered one very important story idea I wanted to talk to you about."

Theresa frowned. "Stevie, I thought I told you—"

"But wait!" Stevie insisted, leaning forward and gripping the edge of the table. "I really think you'll be interested in this. Have you ever heard of Pine Hollow Stables?"

"Sure." Theresa shrugged. "That's the riding place just outside of town, right? But what does that have to do with—"

"I've been riding there for years," Stevie plowed on, ignoring the slightly annoyed expression on Theresa's face. "And one of the most wonderful traditions at Pine Hollow is something called the Starlight Ride." Without waiting for an invitation, she quickly outlined the basics. "You reminded me about it when you were talking about the Fenton Hall anniversary thing just now. Um, because the Starlight Ride is an important, totally cherished tradition, just like attending our school is." She realized that was sort of a stretch, but she let it stand, holding her breath as she watched Theresa's face.

The editor was nodding thoughtfully. "Hmmm," she said. "That does sound sort of interesting. And quite a few of our readers are riders. . . . All right, Stevie." Theresa smiled. "Let's do it."

Stevie let out an excited whoop. "Really? I can do the article?"

"You can do the article," Theresa confirmed. "On two conditions."

"Sure!" Stevie agreed immediately, figuring that Theresa probably wanted to assign another reporter to give her some tips. Or maybe she thought Stevie needed a research assistant of her own.

"Number one, I'll need the finished article next Thursday at the latest," Theresa said. "That week will be our last issue before winter break, and there's not much point in running a holiday article in January."

"No problem," Stevie said quickly. "What's number two?"

"Number two, you should only take this on if you're sure it won't interfere with your work with Cassidy."

Stevie's heart plummeted like a stone. "O-Oh," she stammered. Obviously, it wasn't going to be quite as easy as she'd hoped to get out of research duty. But what else could she say, especially now that Theresa was being so nice about the Starlight Ride idea? "Um, sure. No problem there, either."

"Good." Theresa glanced at the clock above the door. "I guess that's it for now, then. You can talk to Cassidy today at our regular staff meeting and make arrangements directly with her. The homeroom bell's about to ring—you'd better get going. See you at the meeting."

Stevie said good-bye and hurried out of the media room, a little relieved to be escaping without any mention of writing up lunch menus or spell-checking teachers' names. *Okay, so maybe I'm still stuck playing research assistant,* she thought with a mixture of annoyance and resignation. *But at least now I also have a real story to keep me excited about this whole newspaper thing.*

Carole clenched the wheel of her car as she took the familiar turn into Pine Hollow's small gravel parking lot. She'd been growing steadily more nervous ever since she'd left school a few minutes earlier. Scanning the cars already in the lot, she immediately spotted an unfamiliar one, a recent-model black Jeep. It had to be Cam's.

Hopping out of her car, Carole dropped her keys in her coat pocket and then smoothed a wrinkle out of her newest pair of navy breeches, which she'd changed into in the bathroom before leaving school. Even though she wouldn't have thought twice about riding in jeans with Cam before—and even though she still wasn't sure whether this was a real date or just a casual ride—Carole couldn't help wanting to look her best.

She didn't see any sign of Cam in the stable yard. Denise McCaskill was talking to a couple of adult riding students over near the schooling ring, though. Giving the pretty, petite stable manager a quick wave as she hurried past, Carole entered the main building through the big wooden doors. Blinking quickly to help her eyes adjust to the relatively dim artificial light after the brilliant autumn sunshine outside, she glanced around and then headed across the entryway. A quick check of the student locker room, tack room, and office failed to turn up any sign of Cam. Wandering back into the main entryway, Carole stopped in the middle, wondering where he could be. Maybe she'd been wrong about the Jeep—maybe it belonged to one of Max's adult students and Cam hadn't arrived yet.

Suddenly she had an idea. If their positions were switched, where would she be? She certainly wouldn't be wasting time hanging around an empty entryway. *No way,* she thought, already turning to hurry toward the nearest end of the U-shaped stable aisle. *I would have headed straight for the horses. And maybe Cam's changed a little since the old days, but he can't have changed* that *much.*

Sure enough, as soon as she entered the long arm of the first aisle, she spotted Cam leaning on the half door of a stall a few yards ahead, rubbing the nose of a friendly old gelding named Patch. Carole's stomach lurched nervously again.

Wrapping her arms around her waist, she hesitantly called Cam's name. *I have to figure out what's happening here before it gives me an ulcer or something,* she thought, pasting a smile on her face. He turned and spotted her, a grin lighting up his handsome features. *I've got to know whether I'm just a pal to him, a blast from the past, or if maybe he's hoping for something more.*

Cam gave her a clue right away by hurrying over and greeting her with a tight, lingering hug. "Hi," he whispered directly into her ear, his warm breath tickling her skin. "I was waiting for you." Carole hugged him back, wondering if it was normal for her stomach to be jumping around like a rambunctious colt kicking up its heels on a sunny spring day. Her throat was giving her trouble now, too. It couldn't seem to make a sound as long as Cam's strong arms were wrapped around her that way.

As she pulled away from the embrace, Carole caught movement out of the corner of her eye. Glancing toward the end of the aisle, she saw a familiar figure coming toward them, leading a tall, solidly built bay gelding. Ben Marlow.

Carole gulped. If she'd been uncomfortable before, it had just been multiplied by about a thousand. As usual, Ben's face revealed little about what he was thinking, but Carole caught his dark eyes darting nervously from side to side and guessed that he was also feeling awkward.

"Um, h-hi, Ben," Carole stammered uncertainly, glancing from one guy to the other. She couldn't help being struck by the stark differences between them. Cam looked relaxed and pleasant as always, a smile already forming on his handsome face as he watched Ben approach. For his part, Ben kept his gaze trained steadily on his horse, his face as impassive as a block of ice. Carole winced, wishing that for just once he would at least try to be as friendly and caring with the two-legged variety of mammals around Pine Hollow as he was with the four-legged types. "Uh, this is my old friend Cam. Cam Nelson. Cam, this is Ben Marlow."

"Nice to meet you," Cam said politely. He took a step toward Ben, starting to extend his hand. At that moment, the horse Ben was leading suddenly let out a loud snort and tossed his head violently. Cam jumped back, startled, and laughed nervously.

Meanwhile, Ben had turned all his attention to the horse. Carole felt her cheeks burn. She could never prove it, but she couldn't help suspecting that Ben had done something to make the horse, a normally placid gelding named Windsor, act up at that precise moment.

Don't be stupid, she chided herself. *Why would he do that?*

She tugged at Cam's sleeve. "Come on," she said, doing her best to sound normal. "Want to say hi to Starlight?"

As they turned away, Ben moved on. As soon as he'd disappeared around the corner, Cam raised one eyebrow and looked down at Carole. "Wow," he said. "Is it just me, or is that guy definitely the strong, silent type?"

Carole smiled weakly. "He gets really focused on his work, I guess. Now come on—let's hit the tack room. We'll stop off in the office on our way and sign you up to ride Diablo. Okay?"

"Lead the way." Cam gave a little bow and gestured her forward.

Not too long after that, the two of them were tacked up and mounted in the stable yard. Carole was happy to see that Cam's recent lack of practice hadn't hurt him much—he still had a terrific seat and his hands on Diablo's reins were sure and firm. Soon they were riding out of the stable yard side by side, heading toward the woods beyond the big south pasture, where several of Carole's favorite trails began.

Carole had expected the familiar activity of riding across the fields to calm her nerves, at least a little. But instead her stomach was bucking and twisting more than ever. Still, she did her best to focus on Starlight and on the pleasant, sunny afternoon.

Eventually it worked. She started to relax. By the time she and Cam rode into the dappled shade of the woods, they were chatting easily. Once again Carole found herself talking away like she might never stop. Cam always seemed to have an interesting question or comment for her, and just when she thought they would run out of things to talk about, she would think of something else she wanted to ask him or share with him.

She wasn't even sure how much time had passed when they reached the part of the trail that followed the meandering course of the narrow, babbling brook that had given the town of Willow Creek its name. Soon the trail narrowed, forcing them to ride single file. Carole let Cam go first. She was glad that they were moving at a walk, since she was really having trouble staying focused on her horse and the trail. Her gaze kept straying back to the same place: Cam's broad, strong back. She still couldn't quite get over just how good-looking Cam was now, and now that they couldn't really talk much, she once again started to feel anxious and a little awed that he wanted to spend time with her.

I don't know what I'm getting so worked up about, though, really, she told herself, adjusting her balance automatically as Starlight moved around a slight bend in the trail. *It's not like he's really given me any serious indication that he wants to be anything more than friends. And why should he? I'm just getting my hopes up because he's looking so fine these days and it's gone to my head.*

After thinking about that for another minute or two, she almost had herself convinced. Seeing Ben back there at the stable had reminded her of just how clueless she could be about guys and their intentions. After all, hadn't she practically gone into orbit after Ben had kissed her at that horse show last month? It had been a huge surprise, but that hadn't stopped her from making all kinds of assumptions about his feelings. She had totally misread him though, obviously, since he hadn't so much as alluded to that kiss since then. How likely was it that Carole was doing the same thing again now, assuming too much just because Cam acted happy to see her again?

"Hey, check it out," Cam called over his shoulder, gesturing at a wide part of the creek. "That looks like a good place to give the horses a rest and a drink."

Carole nodded and pulled up her horse, swung herself out of the saddle, and then led Starlight off the trail. Cam did the same with Diablo, and soon they were standing side by side between the two drinking horses.

Cam glanced over at her. "This is nice," he said, his voice so soft that Carole could barely hear him over the slurping sounds Starlight and Diablo were making as they quenched their thirst.

She nodded, feeling shy. They were standing awfully close together, the horses' big bodies seeming to shelter them from the rest of the world. "Yes," she said. "I'm glad we—*ulp!*"

The last exclamation slipped out when Cam took a step closer and put his right arm around her shoulders. She stared up at him, frozen in surprise and bewilderment.

"I'm so glad I came back," Cam murmured, gazing into her eyes as his arm tightened around her. The horses continued to drink, oblivious to what their riders were up to, as Cam squeezed Carole's shoulder gently. "It was worth moving all the way across the country to get a chance to know you again."

Carole's mind raced. She wanted to come up with an intelligent response—something to show him that she felt the same way—but her brain seemed to be moving in slow motion.

Cam didn't seem to mind. Loosening Diablo's lead a little more, he raised his left hand and pushed back the brim of her hard hat. Then he slipped his hand behind her neck, pulling her toward him.

Yikes! Carole thought frantically. *Is he going to—*

Before she could finish the thought, Cam kissed her. Carole found herself kissing him back, her body relaxing into his embrace. After a moment, Cam pulled away and looked at her, his dark eyes serious and thoughtful.

Uh-oh, here it comes. Carole steeled herself as her stomach dipped nervously. *This is where he mumbles something unintelligible and makes an excuse to take off.*

She was only half serious, but it was still a bit of a surprise when instead of releasing her, Cam touched her softly on the chin. "You really are beautiful," he whispered. "You know that, don't you?" Without waiting for a reply, he leaned down and kissed her again.

This time Carole didn't think anything at all. She was hardly even aware that Starlight had finished his drink and was slobbering icy water down her back. She felt like a character in a movie—a wonderful romance film with a happy ending—and all she wanted to do was enjoy it.

FIVE

A blast of chilly wind propelled Lisa through the glass entryway. She took a deep breath of the warm, faintly pine-scented air and glanced around, unzipping her coat.

Just a few weeks before Christmas, the mall was a frenzy of blinking lights, fake greenery, and red-and-green bunting. It was also crowded: People of all shapes, sizes, and ages hurried along every which way, most of them loaded down with packages. The sounds of various holiday songs playing tinnily in the surrounding stores was all but drowned out by the hordes of people talking, laughing, arguing. Somewhere not too far away, an unseen baby was crying in a high-pitched whine. Just a few yards ahead of Lisa, in the broad plaza surrounding a holly-bedecked fountain, two toddlers were chasing each other back and forth, shrieking in a tone that Lisa would have thought only dogs should be able to hear. For a moment she was tempted to turn around and head right back out to her car, which was wedged into a too-small parking spot at the very end of the second-to-last row of the lot.

But she resisted the urge. *This will be good for me,* she thought determinedly. *I can get a little last-minute Christmas shopping done, maybe buy myself a present to cheer myself up. I could use a new pair of earrings to wear with my blue dress on Friday.*

Somehow the thought of accessorizing didn't excite her much. She wasn't even sure whether to look forward to the CARL fund-raising party or not. On the one hand, it would be a great chance to get out and have some fun with her friends instead of sitting at home alone as she'd done much of the previous weekend. And she already knew that Alex wouldn't be there—Stevie had told her that. But she also didn't relish the thought of hanging around some crowded party without Alex at her side, making her laugh, being glad that she was with him and making her feel loved and appreciated.

Still, she had to move on sometime. It had been her idea to take a break from their relationship, and the agreement had been that they would stay away from each other for the next few weeks—and that they would see other people in the meantime. Maybe if she survived going stag to the CARL event, she'd start thinking about going out with an actual other guy on an actual date sometime soon. Maybe she would even work up the courage to ask someone out the following weekend.

She felt a stab of intense guilt and sadness at the very thought. What would Alex say if he knew she was thinking this way? If he found out she was getting ready to move on to other guys before they'd been broken up a week?

Forget about Alex, Lisa told herself firmly, dodging around a portly woman pushing a baby carriage piled high with shopping bags and packages. There was no baby in sight. *No matter what I decide about dating, I definitely can't just keep moping around the house—not unless I want to turn into Mom.*

Shuddering slightly, she plunged forward into the sea of humanity, making her way by memory toward a small store beyond the fountain plaza that sold costume jewelry and other small accessories.

"Welcome to Accessorama," a tired-looking woman dressed as an elf said perfunctorily as Lisa finally pushed and dodged her way to the store entrance. "May your holidays sparkle like rhinestones."

"Thank you," Lisa responded politely, feeling sorry for the woman. She knew what a thankless job it was working in a retail store during the holiday shopping season—her mother worked at a clothing store at the other end of the mall, and she had just about had a nervous breakdown the year before during the pre-Christmas rush.

Of course, that shouldn't be a problem this year, Lisa reminded herself ruefully, thinking of the way her mother had been calling in sick left and right ever since her loser boyfriend had dumped her right after Thanksgiving. *There's no chance of her getting over-worked these days. The only real danger is that she won't have a job at all come the New Year. It will be a real Christmas miracle if her boss doesn't sack her after this.*

She tried not to think about what would happen if her mother really did lose her job. There wasn't much Lisa could do about it one way or the other.

After browsing in the shop for a few minutes, Lisa decided to move on. She didn't see any earrings she liked there, and besides, she really did want to do some shopping for her friends. She'd already bought Stevie a bracelet, but she still needed to find a Christmas gift for Carole. Fortunately, Carole wasn't hard to shop for. After leaving Accessorama with a sympathetic smile for the woman at the entrance, she headed straight for the tack shop a few stores farther down the mall. She figured she could find something there for Carole, and also for the other people at Pine Hollow. Lisa always liked to buy a little something for Max and his family, and for the past couple of years she'd also exchanged gifts with Red and Denise.

As soon as Lisa stepped into The Saddlery, the scents of leather and saddle soap surrounded her, replacing the aroma of pine and peppermint that permeated the rest of the mall. She breathed in deeply, enjoying the pleasant, slightly spicy smell as she surveyed the store, but then let out the breath in a surprised *whoosh* when she spotted a familiar face at the checkout counter. It was George Wheeler, and he was setting a pile of items in front of the cashier.

Lisa was tempted to duck out of the shop again before he saw her—she'd never quite felt comfortable around George. He had a weird way of staring at people just a little too long that she found rather unsettling. But she felt guilty for the thought. *This is supposed to be the season of fellowship and good cheer, right?* she said to herself. *So let's do some season's greetings.*

"Lisa! Hi!" George said in surprise when she tapped him on the shoulder. As he smiled at her, she noticed a faint smudge of something brown—chocolate ice cream?—on one round, pink cheek. "What are you doing here?"

"Shopping," Lisa said lamely, forcing a smile as George laughed as if it were the funniest thing anyone had ever said. "How about you?"

"Oh, you know." George winked, or at least that was what Lisa assumed he was trying to do. One eye closed completely, while the other twitched halfway shut. "Just doing the Santa thing."

"Hmmm." Lisa was getting ready to move on when she glanced down at the items on the counter. The cashier had turned away to run George's credit card through the machine, and she hadn't bagged his purchases yet. Along with several small items—a snaffle bit, a pair of grooming gloves, a tube of leather conditioner—Lisa noticed a gorgeous tweed hunt coat. "Wow! Are you buying this?" She glanced at him uncertainly, wondering if he realized it was a woman's garment. With George, you couldn't take these things for granted—he wasn't exactly the king of fashion, as evidenced by his wrinkled blue pants and striped button-down.

George smiled coyly. "Oh, yes," he replied, giving her his sort-of wink again. "This is for someone very special."

For a second Lisa was relieved that he wasn't buying the coat for himself. Then she gulped as she realized what his words might mean. *Someone very special? I wonder if that means Callie.* She thought back, trying to remember if Stevie had told her anything about George's crush on Callie lately. *I thought that was all over.* She gaze at the expensive coat. *But it looks like maybe George didn't get the memo.*

"Okay," Lisa said to George. "Well, I'll see you around."

"Bye, Lisa," George said distractedly as the cashier returned with the credit slip for him to sign. "See you."

Lisa moved on farther into the store, glancing around at the well-stocked shelves and waiting for inspiration to strike. It didn't take long. Within five minutes, she'd found a horse-shaped picture frame for Red and Denise and a set of equine-themed Christmas ornaments for Max and his wife Deborah, as well as stuffed ponies for their two young daughters. A moment later she found an embroidered sweatshirt that she was sure Carole would love. Holding it up, she stared at it blankly, imagining what Carole would do if, say, Ben Marlow bought her something as extravagant as the fancy tweed coat George was buying for Callie.

And let's not kid ourselves here, Lisa thought, tucking the sweatshirt under her arm and heading for the cashier. *It's for Callie, whether he admits it or not. No doubt about that. The only question remaining is, do I warn her, or do I mind my own business?*

She was still trying to decide what to do when she left the tack shop a few minutes later, her carefully wrapped gifts in a large shopping bag printed with the store logo. The dry, overheated mall air was making her thirsty, so she decided to grab a soda before she continued her shopping. She had almost reached the food court, which was just as crowded as the rest of the mall, when she heard someone calling her name. Turning, she saw A.J. McDonnell heading toward her, waving.

"Hey!" Lisa called, a little surprised to see him. Like Phil Marsten, A.J. lived in Cross County, about ten miles away. It was unusual to see anyone from Cross County at the Willow Creek Mall unless they were meeting someone there, since there was a much nicer mall on the other side of Cross County in a town called Berryville. "What are you doing here?"

A.J. shrugged and didn't answer for a moment.

Then he seemed to change his mind. "I just had a session. The office is in the business park on the other side of the parking lot, so I thought I'd stop in here and grab something to eat."

"Oh." Lisa didn't ask any more questions. She knew that A.J. had been seeing someone to work through his problems—the adoption, the drinking—and figure out how to deal with them. She just hoped it was doing some good. She missed the old, happy-go-lucky A.J. "I was just about to get a soda myself. Want to join me?"

"Sure."

The two of them headed to the nearest counter, a hot dog place, and bought drinks and an order of curly fries to share. By a stroke of sheer luck, they managed to snag a small table when a pair of elderly women got up to leave, and soon they were seated across from each other, munching on their snack.

Lisa noticed that A.J. didn't seem to have much to say. In fact, he kept staring into his soda with a little frown, stirring it with his straw but not really drinking it. "Is something wrong?" Lisa asked at last. "Is your soda okay?"

A.J. looked up at her and blinked. "What?"

"I said, are you all right?" Lisa was starting to think that there might be more to her friend's unhappy expression than soda. A.J.'s lightly freckled face wore the same distracted, closed expression that it had taken on soon after he'd found out about his adoption, when he had stopped communicating with just about everyone.

To her surprise, he sighed and answered. "Now that you mention it, no, I'm *not* all right. Julianna and I broke up today."

"What?" Lisa was startled. "Oh, A.J., I'm sorry. What happened?" She tried to keep her voice calm, though inside she was seething. She'd always worried about how deeply A.J. adored Julianna. She was fun-loving and outgoing and very, very pretty. In Lisa's opinion, she was also a tad shallow and self-centered. Though Lisa didn't mind having Julianna around, she'd always been a bit cautious about really befriending her, fearing that the flirtatious redhead would hurt A.J. someday—dump him for a better-looking or more popular guy, or maybe just because she'd become bored. But Lisa hadn't thought that anyone—even someone like Julianna—would kick a guy when he was already so low.

"We'd made plans to hang out for a while before my session," A.J. explained, picking at a clod of dried mustard on the table. "That's when I told her I couldn't see her anymore."

Lisa was startled. "*You* broke up with *her*? Why?" A.J. had dumped Julianna once before, back when he'd been in the midst of the most painful feelings about his family and thought he just couldn't handle a girlfriend at the same time. But that had been a while ago, and Lisa thought he'd come past that stage.

A.J. shrugged and stirred his soda again. "She's still drinking," he said quietly. "She brought a bottle of tequila along today—and that was the last straw."

"Oh." Lisa did her best to take that in. She knew that Julianna had done some drinking right along with A.J., but she had assumed she had only done it to stay close to him. She never would have dreamed that Julianna's drinking would have continued after A.J.'s had stopped.

"I can't be around that right now," A.J. continued, looking anxious. He ran one hand over his reddish brown hair and glanced around the food court. "It's hard enough just—well, you know. Without dealing with someone else's issues, too."

Lisa nodded slowly, a little surprised by A.J.'s resolve but proud, too. It wouldn't do him or Julianna any good if he tried to help her and ended up in even deeper trouble himself instead. "I understand," she told him sincerely. "And if Julianna's acting that way, it was probably the smartest thing to do."

A.J. smiled, looking relieved. Lisa wondered if he'd been having doubts about his decision. She wondered if he blamed himself for Julianna's drinking and felt guilty about it. "Thanks," he said. "But listen. Don't tell anyone, okay?" He gazed at her beseechingly. "I only told you because, well, I thought you'd understand. You know?"

Lisa guessed that meant he'd heard about her new arrangement with Alex. "I'll keep quiet if you want me to. But are you sure you don't want anyone else to know?" she asked gently. "It's not like you can keep this a secret forever."

A.J. frowned briefly, then relaxed and shrugged. "I guess you're right," he muttered. "They'll probably find out soon anyway. Julianna isn't exactly the most discreet person in the world."

That was true enough. Lisa thought briefly about the vivacious girl and wondered what was going on with her. But she didn't spend long worrying about it. That was a problem for Julianna's family and friends. Lisa's first concern was A.J., and she wanted him to know that she supported him. She also wished she knew a way to make him feel better. His pain was evident on his face. "I have an idea," she said suddenly. "Did Phil tell you about the CARL thing this Friday?"

A.J. shrugged. "Maybe. Is that the party he's going to with Stevie?"

Lisa nodded and filled him in on the details. "The tickets are kind of steep, but it's for a great cause," she finished. "And we're all going—Carole and I were planning to go together, since we don't have dates." She willed herself to keep smiling as said it. "Want to come along with us?"

A.J. hesitated, and for a moment Lisa was sure he was going to say no. But finally he nodded. "Maybe," he said. "I'll think about it. I'm sure my folks would spring for the ticket." He smiled, though his expression was strangely sad. "There's not much they wouldn't do for me these days if I asked."

Carole was still feeling rather light-headed when Cam called for a stop. They had reached one of Carole's favorite picnic spots, a pretty, sunny clearing overlooking a natural pool formed by a bend in the creek. For the first time, Carole remembered that Cam had tied a cantle pack onto his saddle as they'd started out. She'd asked what it was, but he had merely winked and said she'd see when the time was right. Despite his cryptic response, the scent of cookies drifting up from the pack had answered the question clearly enough. Now, Carole's stomach grumbled eagerly as she hopped down from the saddle.

"How did you remember this place was here?" she asked shyly, realizing that Cam had guided their path without her quite noticing that he was doing it. She had planned for them to ride up the hilly trail to the scenic overlook at the edge of the state forest, and yet somehow, here they were, miles from that overlook, in the perfect place for a private picnic.

Cam glanced over his shoulder as he dismounted. "I never forget a beautiful spot where I spent time with a beautiful woman," he replied.

Carole wasn't sure which flustered her more—

being called beautiful again or being referred to as a woman. She still thought of herself as very much a girl. *Still, if Cam wants to call me a beautiful woman, I guess I shouldn't object,* she thought as she led Starlight to a patch of still-green grass nearby.

Soon both horses were munching contentedly and Cam was carefully spreading a checkered wool blanket on the ground near the creek. Once again, Carole had the weird feeling that she was a character in a movie, taking part in some picture-perfect romance. The feeling made her a little uncomfortable, but she was also starting to like it. Removing her hard hat, she shook out her hair and wished she'd remembered to stick some lip gloss in her pocket. Wetting her lips with her tongue, she shifted her weight from one foot to the other, wondering what she was supposed to do now.

"Have a seat," Cam said as if reading her mind, patting a spot on the blanket as he turned to rustle through his pack. "I'll have everything ready in just a sec."

Carole obeyed, sinking to the ground and watching as he unpacked cheese and crackers, a small basket of juicy red strawberries, cookies, a bottle of mineral water, and even a stout scented candle, which he lit with a flourish. "There," he said with satisfaction. "I think that's everything—no, wait. There's something missing." He scratched his head, pretending to be confused, though Carole thought she detected a twinkle in his eye. Suddenly he said, "Aha!" and grabbed his bag again. Reaching inside, he pulled out a single red rose and presented it to her. "For you."

Carole gasped. She couldn't believe her eyes. Nobody had ever made such a romantic gesture for her before. Her fingers trembled slightly as she accepted the flower. "Thank you," she said, though the words seemed inadequate. "Cam, this is all so wonderful. I—"

"No need to thank me," he interrupted, scooting a little closer on the blanket. "Your presence is thanks enough."

Until that moment, Carole hadn't really known what people meant when they said they swooned. But she was starting to understand the feeling. *Is this really happening?* she wondered. *Maybe it's a dream. It certainly feels like a dream. A wonderful, magical, unbelievable dream that makes me never want to wake up.*

Carole had always thought that Cam was really special. He had always treated her well and been a good, caring friend. But not like this. This went above and beyond anything she might have expected. Anything she had ever known before.

Before, I was never even quite sure if we were boyfriend and girlfriend, she thought, selecting a strawberry from the basket Cam was holding up to her. *We didn't really have time to figure that out before his family moved away. But now . . ..*

Despite her earlier worries, Carole had to admit that there wasn't much doubt remaining in her mind. Cam wanted to pick up where they'd left off, and then some. He was treating her like the most desirable girl—no, *woman*—in the world, and he wasn't shy about showing how he felt.

"Carole," Cam said, glancing up from pouring her some mineral water. He'd brought along plastic goblets that looked sort of like wine glasses. "I have something important I want to ask you."

What now? Carole wondered rather giddily as she accepted the plastic goblet and took a sip. *Is he about to propose? Sweep me off to a honeymoon in Paris to top things off?*

She did her best to hold back a giggle at the thought. "Yes, Cam?" she said instead. "What is it?"

"I just need to know," Cam said seriously. "Are you seeing anyone else? Other guys, I mean." He cleared his throat and shrugged. "I—I just want to know if I have any competition I need to worry about."

That swoony feeling was overtaking Carole again. She had the nagging feeling that she should say something witty or clever or coy here. Something flirtatious that would let Cam know that she was sophisticated and sly and a little bit mysterious . . .

But that just wasn't her. Even if she could have thought of some perfect comeback, Carole didn't want to act that way. She didn't want to play games.

She just wanted to let Cam know how much she appreciated how sweet he was being. "No," she said simply, holding his gaze steadily. "I'm not seeing anyone at all."

As Cam smiled, looking pleased, the image of Ben Marlow flashed through Carole's mind. She ignored it. She wasn't dating Ben—that was a laugh. Just because he'd kissed her once . . .

All thoughts of Ben fled from her mind as Cam reached out and gently pulled the rose from her hand. Moving a little closer, he brushed back the hair above her ear and carefully, slowly tucked the flower into her thick curly hair. "There," he said, kissing her forehead softly, then moving away to gaze at her with obvious pleasure. "Perfect."

Now Carole was sure that this had to be some kind of silver-screen romance. And the best part was that Cam didn't even seem to notice or mind that she didn't know any of her lines. He was taking care of everything.

The next few minutes passed in a blur. They ate and drank and talked and somehow, somewhere along the way, Cam moved closer and they held hands. Then Cam's arm found its way around her waist. After that, it seemed almost inevitable that he would pause in midsentence, lock his eyes on hers, and then lean toward her for another kiss.

Carole was slightly startled when he pulled away

this time after only a few seconds. "What?" she gasped, worried that the dream had been too good to last. "What's wrong?"

"Nothing," Cam said huskily, reaching out to straighten the rose, which had slipped partway out of Carole's hair. "I—I just want to say, I don't usually do this. Move this fast, I mean."

"Oh!" Carole hadn't really thought about it that way. Were they moving too fast? Should she be doing something different, trying to slow things down?

"But it's different with you," Cam went on before she could figure it out. He took both her hands in his as they sat there on the blanket facing each other. "I *feel* different with you. You're special, Carole. I—I know I should probably just play it cool, hide my feelings—I don't want to scare you off."

"I'm not scared," Carole whispered breathlessly.

Cam smiled. "Good," he replied. "Because I just can't help myself. You're just as beautiful and wonderful and sweet as I remembered, and more. That's why I want to ask . . ." He paused and took a deep breath. "Carole, will you go steady with me? Please?"

Carole gasped, stunned. But for once, she actually knew the right thing to say. "Yes!" she blurted out, so loudly that Starlight lifted his head and snorted. "Yes, I will!"

Cam laughed in delight. Then he threw his arms around her and hugged her tight. "Great," he said. "That's great!"

Carole laughed, too. She was still laughing when Cam loosened his grip just enough to find her lips again with his own. This time the kiss didn't seem likely to end anytime soon, and Carole for one was happy about that.

Yes, she thought as she sank into a state of sheer bliss, *this is* definitely a *date!*

SIX

"Lisa! Wait up!"

Lisa turned and peered down the crowded school hallway. Carole was racing toward her, her face flushed and happy and papers and books threatening to spill out of her arms at any moment. "Hi," Lisa greeted her friend with a smile. "You look happy. Does this mean the ride yesterday went well?"

"Do horses eat hay?" Carole replied with a grin. "It was fantastic!" She paused and glanced around at the hordes of people in the hall, then grabbed Lisa's arm and dragged her to the relative privacy of the nook beyond the end of the locker row. "Get this," she whispered, her dark eyes shining. "He asked me to go steady!"

Lisa gasped. *Wow,* she thought. *Cam doesn't waste any time!*

She immediately felt a little guilty for the thought. After all, it wasn't as if Carole and Cam were getting to know each other for the first time. They were just getting reacquainted. And apparently they both liked what they were relearning about each other.

Besides, she reminded herself, *it's great that Carole's finally getting some male attention. How many times have Stevie and I asked each other why guys aren't falling all over such a beautiful, kind, talented person? She deserves a little romance in her life. A girl can't live on horses alone, after all. Not even Carole.*

"Congratulations!" she told Carole sincerely, grabbing her friend in a hug and almost knocking her books out of her grip. "That's wonderful. You said yes, I take it?"

"Uh-huh." Carole giggled, hugging her back and then pulling away to straighten her books. "This is so amazing! Now I know how you guys felt when you first got together with your—oops." Her face fell and she gave Lisa an apologetic look. "Sorry, I wasn't thinking."

Lisa forced herself to maintain a cheerful expression. "Don't be silly," she said. "So tell me all about it. How did he ask you?"

Carole launched into the story. Lisa listened, trying not to feel too wistful. *Once upon a time, Alex and I made each other feel that way,* she thought. *So what happened to us? Why can't people just fall in love and then stay like that forever—happy and giddy and floating on air?*

". . . and by the time we remembered the time and

headed back, it was getting late," Carole continued excitedly. "It was already growing dark, and I was due home in, like, fifteen minutes. So Cam"—she paused and let out a contented sigh at his name—"Cam insisted on cooling down and untacking both our horses. He said he didn't want me to miss my curfew, otherwise Dad might not let us go out again, and he couldn't stand that."

"Wow," Lisa said. "Sounds serious."

"I know." Carole clutched her books tighter to her chest. "I feel like I've finally figured out what this thing called romance is all about."

"That's great," Lisa said, trying to sound light-hearted. But something in her voice or expression must have given her away, because Carole sobered immediately.

"I'm sorry, Lisa," she said again. "Here I am going on and on about my date when you—well, anyway, I'm sorry."

"Don't be," Lisa said. "Alex and I will get through this one way or another."

Carole nodded, looking unconvinced. "Anyway," she said tentatively. "Um, I was thinking. About what Stevie was saying the other day." She gazed at Lisa expectantly.

Lisa laughed. "You'll have to be more specific," she teased, leaning against the locker behind her. "Stevie tends to have a lot to say, and sometimes it's hard to keep track."

Carole smiled sheepishly. "Oh, yeah. Um, I meant the stuff she was saying about, you know, asking someone to the CARL thing. Like Scott or whoever."

Lisa frowned. "Oh."

"No, really," Carole went on hurriedly. "I mean, I know she was probably just thinking of her own problems when she suggested it. Mostly, anyway. But maybe it's not such a bad idea, you know? To start out with a guy you know as a friend." She smiled beseechingly. "It's not too late to ask him."

Lisa felt a twinge of annoyance. Why did people who were falling in love always try to fix up everyone they knew, whether they needed it or not?

But then she realized what Carole was really doing. "Oh!" she said. "Did you and Cam want to go? Together, I mean?"

"Oh, I don't know," Carole said quickly, shifting her books from one arm to the other. "I mean, we hadn't really talked about it or anything. Besides, I already said I'd go with you. I'm looking forward to it."

Lisa couldn't help laughing at the half hopeful, half miserable expression on her friend's face. "Don't be silly," she said. "You and Cam should definitely go together. You're a couple now, and that's what couples do."

Carole protested weakly for a moment or two, but Lisa wouldn't budge. Finally Carole gave in. "Well, okay," she said, sounding relieved. "But you're still going to go, right?"

"Of course. I'll tag along with Callie or someone." Lisa shrugged. "Or maybe with Stevie and Phil—they won't mind having me along, especially if A.J. comes with us, too."

"Are you sure?" Carole still looked guilty. "I mean, Scott—"

"I don't think that's such a great idea," Lisa interrupted. "Especially if he really is interested in Stevie. Things could get complicated." She shrugged again. "But don't worry. With a date or without, I'm in for sure. I can't let all those homeless animals down, right? In fact, I was thinking this morning that I'd feel a little guilty using that free ticket you offered. Dad already sent me a nice fat check for Christmas—I can pay for a ticket myself. You and Cam can use the free ones."

Carole started to protest anew at that, but the shrill sound of the bell interrupted her.

"Gotta go," Lisa said. "If anyone's even two seconds late to Spanish, Señora Torres makes them sing Spanish folk songs in front of the whole class."

She waved good-bye to Carole and hurried off, her mind already on the upcoming CARL event. *This is definitely weird,* she thought, stepping around a teacher who was scolding a couple of guys in the middle of the hall. *I'm not used to being the one who's stuck without a date for the big party.*

She wondered if she was feeling anything like the way Carole must have felt many times over the years,

128

when Lisa and Stevie were busy with their boyfriends and Carole was the one without a date. Maybe that was why Carole had always been able to focus so strongly on horses—her one true, faithful love.

And maybe that's not such a bad thing in some ways, Lisa thought as she reached her classroom and headed in to take her seat. *Carole is so totally dedicated, so focused. She knows exactly what she wants to do with her life.*

Could Lisa gain that kind of focus now that she didn't have a boyfriend taking up so much of her time? Maybe if she took some real time off from dating, she could whip her life into shape and figure out her own future.

Tapping her fingers on her desk, Lisa glanced around the room. The teacher was up by her desk, talking to a couple of girls, so everyone else was relaxing, chatting, or rushing to finish their homework before class started.

Lisa surveyed the guys in the class. Could she really imagine herself dating any of them? Talking with them, waiting for them to pick her up, kissing them good night? She shook her head. It felt so strange even to think about such a thing.

She turned her thoughts to Alex. He and Lisa were supposed to get together at the end of the month and talk, figure out where to go from there. All along, she'd been assuming that they would get back together. But now, as she tried to picture what the reunion would be like, she had trouble bringing it into focus. What would he say about their time apart? What would she want him to say?

She sighed and leaned her elbows on her desk, resting her chin on her hand as the teacher finally called the class to order. Once again, her mind returned to the other option. *I could just swear off guys entirely,* she told herself. *Spend the next eight months studying and spending time with my friends and getting to know myself, on my own. Alone. Totally solo.*

The idea was frightening and strangely appealing at the same time. What would it be like, going through the rest of the year in this sort of dating limbo? How would she fill her time?

She wasn't sure. Giving up dating entirely seemed kind of extreme, but she didn't think the other possibilities were all that appealing, either. Still, whatever she decided to do, she knew one thing for sure: She didn't want to end up like her mother, feeling as if she had no life at all without a man by her side.

". . . and then the main character in the movie hijacked this parade horse, which was actually this awesome Arabian mare with super conformation and tons of spirit. She ran like she never wanted to stop," George said cheerfully. "As soon as I saw her, I said, that's exactly the kind of horse Callie would love to find for herself. Too bad it was just a TV show, huh?"

Callie gritted her teeth, wishing that their chemistry teacher hadn't decided to let them break into their lab groups to work on their next project. The class had started only ten minutes earlier, and George was already wearing on her last nerve. *Why can't he get the hint?* she wondered in frustration. *Why doesn't he realize that I meant it when I said we needed to take a break from our friendship?*

"Anyway, enough about me," George burbled, oblivious to Callie's growing impatience. "What's new with you? How's your training going?"

Callie took a deep breath, ready to explode and tell him off, once and for all, no holds barred. Just in time, she noticed the teacher wandering up and down the aisle nearby and remembered where they were. *This isn't the time or the place,* she told herself firmly, doing her best to keep her fury under control. *It can wait. I'll take care of it later—if I survive this class, that is.*

"I haven't had much time for training," she blurted out, desperate to distract herself from her anger and frustration. "I've been too busy running all over the county looking at horses. And I'm still at it. I have, like, four appointments set up already this week. I'm seeing a couple of Arabians on Wednesday at a farm Denise recommended, and then on Thursday I'm checking out a nice-sounding Appy over at that place on Highway Twelve. Of course, if experience tells me anything, he'll probably turn out to be lame in three legs and half donkey besides. Or at least half quarter horse." She forced a laugh that sounded tinny and fake in her own ears.

I'm not sure how much longer I can do this, she thought grimly as George started babbling about some wonderful quarter horse he'd ridden once. Lately George seemed to have an uncanny knack for choosing the exact wrong times to start acting like her best friend. If he wasn't stopping to chat with her at the stable in front of Max or other people, he was offering to help her with her schoolwork in front of a teacher so that she couldn't say no.

Luckily, at that moment their chemistry teacher called for attention and started explaining something at the board, putting an end to George's monologue for the rest of the period. When the bell finally rang, releasing them from class, Callie jumped up, gathered her books, and hurried out of the room as fast as she could, ignoring George's calls to wait up.

Running away from him made her feel helpless and a little stupid, but what else could she do? She just had to get away from George's breathless, eager, slightly high-pitched voice and those watery, pale grayish eyes that never seemed to look away from her.

I was sure that little speech the other day about taking a break would work. What else can I do to get through to him? What else can I say? Just then she saw Alex Lake coming down the hall. She almost called hello to him, but then she noticed that he was walking hand in hand with Nicole Adams. Both of them were laughing and looking very content with life. Callie raised one eyebrow, remembering what Stevie had told her about her brother's arrangement with Lisa. *Hmmm,* she added to herself. *Maybe I should give that little speech another try. It certainly seems to be working for Alex and Lisa.*

SEVEN

Stevie rubbed her eyes, wondering if it was actually physically possible to die of boredom. Feeling slightly guilty for the thought, she glanced over at the girl sitting beside her at the heavy oak library table. Cassidy Clark was bent over a thick, yellowed book, her finger moving rapidly across the page as she scanned the words. *Wow,* Stevie thought in amazement. *You'd think she was reading some fascinating bestseller or something, instead of a bunch of dusty old yearbooks and school records and stuff.*

Stifling a yawn, Stevie flipped another page in the old yearbook on the table in front of her. Sneaking a peek at her watch, she sighed. Why did sitting in the Fenton Hall library always seem to make time stand still? Stevie glanced around at the ancient, mismatched, uncomfortable furniture, the crowded stacks, and the oppressively low ceiling. The tiny, narrow windows behind the librarian's desk hardly allowed any sunlight to enter, leaving the task of illumination to be the long, bare, humming fluorescent tubes overhead.

Who could possibly think that anyone could ever get any work done in a depressing place like this? she wondered, not for the first time. *It's no wonder we're practically the only ones here.*

"Here's something interesting," Cassidy said, not taking her eyes off her book. "Says here that Headmaster Fenton—you know, Miss Fenton's uncle, the one who started the school—wanted the school colors to be green and white, just like his mother's family crest, but he let the students vote, and that's why they're crimson and gold instead."

"Yeah. Fascinating," Stevie replied, trying to keep the sarcasm out of her voice.

Cassidy didn't seem to hear her comment. Pulling her large yellow notepad toward her, the senior jotted down some notes, adding to the neatly written list of information that already covered nearly four pages, and then returned to her reading. With another sigh, Stevie did the same—after a guilty glance at her own messy but still mostly blank tablet.

As she turned another page in the yearbook, Stevie found the student superlatives page. *Hmmm,* she thought, scanning it with a twinge of interest. *Let's see who the class standouts were back in 1967.* She recognized the student voted Most Likely to Succeed as her family's orthodontist, and the Best-Dressed Girl had a familiar name and face, too—Stevie was pretty sure the slender, haughty girl in the picture, an older and decidedly less slender woman now, had lived on her block until a few years earlier.

Then she glanced at the Class Clown photo and smiled. The student in the picture was doing a handstand with shoes on his hands and gloves on his feet. Even though the boy had curly blond hair and a big nose, he reminded her a little of A.J. It was something about his expression—goofy, friendly, eager to laugh and have fun.

Of course, A.J. doesn't look that way too often anymore, she thought ruefully, staring at the photo and thinking about what Lisa had told her on the phone the evening before about seeing A.J. at the mall. *I just hope Lisa convinced him to come to the CARL thing on Friday. It would be good for him to get out and have fun, especially right now.*

She still had trouble believing that A.J. had broken up with Julianna. First Lisa and Alex, now A.J. and Julianna—it was starting to feel like an epidemic.

Well, maybe not quite, Stevie admitted, flipping another page and staring at pictures of a long-ago prom. *We can't forget Carole and her long-lost Prince Charming, can we?*

She smiled as she thought about Cam's timely return and the way he'd already swept Carole off her feet, asking her to go steady on their second date. Lisa had filled her in on that little bombshell as well, and Stevie was thrilled. For one thing, she'd always liked Cam. Besides that, Carole had recently confessed to Stevie and Lisa that she was having feelings for Ben Marlow. In typical Carole fashion, she hadn't quite sorted out what those feelings might be or what she wanted to do about them, and now, thanks to Cam, she wouldn't have to worry about it anymore. And Stevie wouldn't have to worry that Ben was going to break her friend's sensitive heart by being his usual blunt, aloof self.

I can't wait to see Cam and Carole together on Friday, Stevie thought happily, still staring at the dancing couples on the page in front of her. *It's about time Carole found a guy who really appreciates her. Someone who'll shower her with the whole roses-and-moonlight deal.*

Thinking about moonlight distracted her for a moment, reminding her of the Starlight Ride. So far she hadn't done more than scribble a few vague notes for her big story. She knew she had to find time to work on it soon. Maybe she could start by interviewing people at school who'd taken lessons at Pine Hollow at one time or another. She was sure Lorraine Olsen would have some nice memories of the Starlight Ride, along with Betsy Cavanaugh and Anna McWhirter. And then there was—

"Look who's here, working her way up from the bottom," a snide, self-satisfied voice interrupted her thoughts.

Stevie glanced up with a scowl. "What do you want, Veronica? I'm busy."

Veronica didn't answer for a moment, though she regarded Stevie with cool amusement. Stevie frowned at her, wondering what was going on. Back when Veronica had ridden regularly at Pine Hollow, she and Stevie had been at each other's throats constantly. A couple of years earlier Veronica had decided that guys were a lot more interesting than horses, and since then, she and Stevie had pretty much stayed out of each other's way.

Then Stevie had featured Veronica in her first article for the *Sentinel*. She just hadn't been able to resist some pretty unflattering references, even though she knew that Veronica would have a cow. Veronica might not care much about her schoolwork or other people's feelings, but she definitely cared about her reputation. Sure enough, Veronica had sworn horrible revenge as soon as the issue came out.

Finally Veronica responded to Stevie's question, her voice serene and almost affable. "Oh, I just thought I'd stop by and give you the latest scoop." She smirked and tossed her shiny dark hair over one shoulder. "The *Sentinel* has a new columnist. And you're looking at her."

Stevie rolled her eyes. "Yeah, right."

Cassidy was looking from one girl to the other, perplexed. "What are you saying, Veronica?" the senior asked curiously. "Did you really decide to join the paper?"

"Well, I didn't so much *decide*. It was more like Theresa begged me to come on board," Veronica replied smugly. "I'm going to be the new gossip columnist." She turned and stared at Stevie, a slightly sinister smile playing around the edges of her carefully lined lips. "And I already have *lots* of ideas for my first column."

Stevie scowled. Was Veronica pulling her leg? Trying to scare her into thinking she was going to write a lot of nasty stuff about Stevie and her friends? If so, it was a pretty weak prank—too lame even for Veronica.

"I'm going to go find out what's going on right now." Stevie jumped to her feet and shot Cassidy an apologetic glance. "Be right back." She hurried out of the library before either of the other girls could say a word.

Moments later, she was leaning on a table in the media room, gaping at Theresa in disbelief. "You can't be serious!" Stevie exclaimed. "You actually gave that—that—that *Veronica* her own column?"

Theresa shrugged, her face registering mild surprise at Stevie's reaction. "When she brought me the idea, I admit I was skeptical at first," the editor said calmly. "A gossip column isn't quite the kind of real news the *Sentinel* usually publishes. But then I thought about it a little and realized that this was a golden opportunity to spice things up a bit, make the paper more fun." She shrugged. "Besides, Veronica seemed like a good choice to write it. She's a pretty influential person at Fenton Hall—you know, socially."

Stevie grimaced. "Only in her own mind," she muttered.

She couldn't believe this was happening. *And the worst part is,* she thought grimly, *it's all my fault. If I hadn't put her in my article, she never would have come up with a stupid idea like this.*

But there didn't seem much point in brooding over that. What was done was done, and Stevie would just have to deal with the consequences. "Are you sure a gossip column is a good idea?" she asked Theresa. "I mean, like you said, it's not really hard-hitting news or anything. What if people take the *Sentinel* less seriously?"

"I don't think that will happen." Theresa didn't seem at all worried about the possibility. "In fact, I think this will make the paper even better. It's good to have a balance. If all you print is hard news or serious, depressing stories, a lot of people aren't going to be as eager to pick it up. That's one reason why most major newspapers have a comics section. And it's why we print nice, happy articles—like the one you're doing on your Christmas trail ride—right along with the more serious, controversial stuff."

Stevie bit her lip. She couldn't really argue with that. What's more, she didn't even necessarily think a gossip column was a terrible idea. In the right hands it could even be a lot of fun. In Veronica's hands, however . . .

"I've got an idea," she blurted out. "What if someone different writes the gossip column every week? That will definitely give it even more of a balance, like you were saying."

Theresa was already shaking her head. "It was Veronica's idea," she said. "She really seems to have a vision for it. I want to give her a chance to do it her way first."

Stevie frowned. Why was Theresa so gung ho to let Veronica do her own thing when she didn't seem willing to give Stevie a chance to do anything except rot away in the moldy depths of the school library? *It's typical,* she thought petulantly. *The rest of us have to work and slave to get what we want. But spoiled brat Veronica gets everything handed to her on a silver platter.*

She didn't think it would help her cause to point that out to Theresa, though, so she bit her tongue. "Okay," she said glumly. "I guess I'd better get back downstairs now. Cassidy needs me."

As she dragged herself out of the media room and headed for the stairwell, Stevie suddenly realized that there was one bright spot to this news, at least. *Veronica is totally Ms. Short Attention Span,* she thought hopefully. *Once she realizes this column-*

writing thing actually requires some real work—the kind that might seriously cut into her shoe-shopping and eyebrow-plucking and guy-scamming time—she'll get sick of it for sure. With any luck, she'll quit the paper and get out of my life again in a week or two, tops.

"Who does this stuff when we're not here?" Carole asked, wrinkling her nose in distaste as she used a dented metal shovel to clean the soiled floor of one of the dog runs.

Craig Skippack glanced over at her from the next run, where he was employed in the same task. "They have a whole staff of volunteers," he explained. "This week, though, most of them are crazed getting ready for the fund-raiser, so I offered to help out with some of the day-to-day stuff as well as the painting and the rest of it."

"Oh." Carole shrugged, deciding that it really wasn't much different from mucking out stalls at Pine Hollow. And at least it was a change of pace from all the painting she'd been doing. She gently pushed aside the resident of her run, an ancient, gray-muzzled cocker spaniel, so that she could get to the garbage bag just outside. "There you go, boy," she told the old dog with a pat on the head when she ducked back inside to make sure she hadn't missed anything. "Nice and clean."

The dog responded by sitting up on its hind legs, panting eagerly and waggling his paws in the air.

Carole laughed with delight. "Look!" she exclaimed. "He can do a trick!" She bent to rub the dog behind the ears, which caused its stub of a tail to wag wildly. "What an old sweetie you are," she crooned. "And so clever, too!"

Craig smiled sadly. "Makes you wonder how he ended up here. Did someone just decide to dump him when he got old or when the family got a new puppy?"

Carole thought that sounded kind of cynical. But then she had to admit that it seemed odd for such a nice old dog to end up in the shelter. "How could anyone not want you?" she murmured, bending down to give the dog a hug. "I don't understand how people can be so selfish."

At that moment the sound of footsteps rang out from the cement-floored hallway outside the runs. Carole glanced up, expecting to see another Hometown Hope worker coming to see how they were doing. Instead, she saw Cam. He was wearing jeans, heavy work boots, and a broad smile.

"Surprise!" he called to her, stopping in front of the dog run. "I thought I'd swing by and see if you guys needed any more help."

Carole gasped and quickly looked over at Craig. "Um, this is my . . . my friend, Cam Nelson," she said shyly. "Is it okay if he helps us out for a while?"

Craig smiled agreeably. "Hey, I'm not going to turn down a volunteer," he said. "Welcome, Cam. Help yourself to a shovel and a garbage bag."

"Will do." Cam grabbed the necessary equipment, then stepped to the door of the run beside Carole's. "Do I just go in? These dogs don't bite, do they?"

"Not in this room," Craig replied, already moving on to the next dirty run. "These are the dogs that are ready for adoption. The behavior problems are in a separate area."

Carole couldn't stop staring at Cam as he let himself into the run. He paused just long enough to scratch its resident, a gangly half-grown mixed-breed puppy, under the chin. She couldn't quite believe he was really there. *And it's not like he's here for the thrill of scraping dog poop off the floor,* she told herself. *He's here because he wants to spend time with me. Me!*

She was so overwhelmed by the idea that she felt tongue-tied, uncertain what to say to this guy—her boyfriend!—now that he was standing there in the flesh. Fortunately Cam didn't seem to be suffering similar problems. He immediately began chatting away as he worked, describing his day at school and telling Carole a funny story about his gym teacher, and before she knew it, she was laughing and chatting right back.

She was so wrapped up in their conversation that she hardly noticed when Craig was called out of the room by another volunteer, leaving her and Cam alone with the dogs. A few minutes later the two of them met in the hallway outside the last set of runs.

"Looks like we're about done here," Cam commented, glancing down the row.

Carole looked, too, and realized he was right. More than a dozen dogs were gazing at them eagerly, tails wagging, from clean runs. She wiped her hands on her jeans and reached for the garbage bag they'd just filled. "I guess we should go find out what we're supposed to do next."

"Okay." Cam stepped closer as she tied off the garbage bag and set it with the others. "But first things first. We never got a chance for a proper hello."

Carole's heart started to pound as she realized what he meant. As Cam dropped his shovel against the wall, Carole tipped her head back. She knew she was supposed to close her eyes—Cam's were closed as his lips touched hers—but she couldn't seem to stop staring at the incredibly handsome, smart, funny guy who was kissing her as if it were the most natural thing in the world.

How did my life change so much in just a couple of days? she wondered giddily, wrapping her arms around Cam's neck. *It's like everything has suddenly gone from black and white to full color.*

She wasn't sure how many minutes had passed when their kiss was interrupted by the clanging sound of someone opening a cage in the next room. Startled, she jumped back. "Oh!" she said. "Um, I guess we should get back to work now."

Cam looked reluctant, but he nodded. "Sure," he said. "Lead the way."

Carole felt self-conscious as she walked down the aisle toward the next room. It was unnerving enough that she could practically feel Cam's eyes on her—crooked braid, grungy jeans, and all—but with fourteen sets of canine eyes following her as well, she really felt like a movie starlet parading in front of an audience with her studly leading man.

"We should probably find Craig," Carole said, figuring that talking was the best way to cover up her weird, jumpy feelings. She started through the surgery room, which was empty at the moment. "He's in charge of the whole group, so he'll be able to tell us where he needs our—*eep!*" Cam had suddenly grabbed her by the shoulders and was pulling her toward one side of the room. "What are you doing?" she asked.

"Shhh!" Cam said with a grin, putting a finger to his lips. "Over here." He pulled her into a large supply closet at one end of the room and shut the door behind them. Only the light coming through the crack under the door allowed her to see Cam gazing down at her. "I just need to be alone with you for a while."

Carole felt a thrill run through her. "Oh!" she breathed, gasping slightly as Cam wrapped his arms around her waist. But then she frowned. "Wait, but we can't," she protested, pushing at his chest as he dipped his head toward her. "We're supposed to be working. The shelter has to be ready by Friday, and they need every person they can—"

Cam cut her off by covering her mouth with his own. Carole knew she should pull away, force him to get back out there and work. There really was a lot to do, and it wasn't fair for them to slack off when the others were counting on them. Not to mention what would happen if they got caught. But somehow, as she sank into his kiss, those things didn't seem quite so important anymore.

"What do you say, boy?" Lisa said as she fastened the buckle on the throatlatch of Topside's bridle. "Ready to head out for a nice quiet trail ride, just the two of us? We don't need anyone else to have fun, right? Just being by ourselves is rewarding in its own way, wouldn't you say?"

The handsome bay gelding didn't seem to have an opinion one way or the other, so Lisa fastened the noseband and then checked over the rest of the tack. She'd been thinking all day about what it meant to be single, and had decided to experiment with enjoying life on her own by going on a solo trail ride. She had already checked in with the stable office, telling Denise where she planned to ride and also making a note on the calendar. That way the stable staff would know approximately what time she'd set out, so that if Topside wasn't back in his stall within a couple of hours, they would know there was trouble. Max wasn't crazy about his riders hitting the trails by themselves, and he didn't allow the younger students to go beyond the stable yard without a partner. But he grudgingly allowed the more advanced riders like Lisa to ride alone as long as they followed the rules.

"There we go," Lisa murmured as she brought the reins over the horse's head, took hold, and got him moving. "Let's head out." She was trying not to feel too weird about what she was doing. It wasn't as if she'd never ridden alone before. But this was different. She wasn't merely working on something she was having trouble with or exercising her horse when her friends weren't available. No, this time she was making a point of going for a pleasure ride all by herself, just for the heck of it.

No big deal, she thought, leading Topside down the aisle toward the entrance. The well-mannered Thoroughbred followed calmly. *Other people do it all the time. Carole doesn't always wait around for someone else to show up and ride with her. Why should I worry about it so much?*

Soon she was mounted up and riding around the schooling ring. On the far side, where the driveway met the hard-packed stable yard, she pulled Topside to a halt, glancing uncertainly from side to side. Should she head across the back fields to one of the wooded trails? Or just circle the front pasture a few times, maybe explore the little patch of trees near the road?

"If I'm going to do this, I might as well do it right," she muttered. She'd written in her note on the calendar that she was planning to take the mountain trail—one of her favorites—and she should just stick with that.

Turning Topside toward the big south pasture, she urged him into a brisk walk. Once they'd gone through the gate, she signaled for a trot and then a canter.

The afternoon was still and cold, but at the relatively fast pace, Lisa's blond hair whipped out behind her, streaming back from beneath the edge of her riding helmet. The air streamed across her cheeks and chin, numbing them slightly and making her eyes water.

Lisa hardly noticed the slight discomfort, though. She had been struck with a sudden joyous, exhilarating feeling of freedom. She realized she didn't have to check with anyone else before changing paces; she didn't have to try to catch up or force herself to wait for anyone. She could change her mind about which trail to take and not have to worry that someone might disagree. It was just her and her horse, free to go wherever they wanted, do whatever they wanted, anytime they wanted. And it felt good.

All too soon, they reached the other end of the

field and entered the woods. Lisa reluctantly pulled Topside back to a walk and the gelding obeyed, though he tossed his head once or twice as if protesting the sedate pace.

"I know how you feel, boy," Lisa said, leaning forward to pat him on the neck. "That was fun, wasn't it?"

She glanced ahead at the well-worn path that wound its way into the woods to the southwest. It had been dubbed the mountain trail years ago by Pine Hollow's riders, though Lisa had always thought that *mountain* was an awfully grand name for the low, time-softened foothills that rose in the forest a few miles from the stable. Over near Cross County, where Phil and A.J. rode, the countryside was wilder and there were some mountains that deserved the name, but as far as Lisa was concerned, Willow Creek's "mountains" were little more than bulges in the landscape. Regardless of the name, Lisa had always been partial to the mountain trail, though her friends preferred the smoother tangle of trails that more or less followed the meanderings of the creek.

Lisa felt herself relaxing as she rode, enjoying the solitude of the winter woods. This late in the fall the calling of birds was sporadic and muted, and most of the time there was no sound at all other than the peaceful rustling of bare branches, the crunching of Topside's hooves moving through dry, drifted fallen leaves, and the horse's deep, even breathing. She'd been riding for nearly half an hour when the silence was marred by the faint sound of voices and laughter from someone ahead of her on the trail. *Oh, great,* Lisa thought with a rueful smile. *Just what I need—a bunch of goofy, giggly intermediate riders wanting to stop and chat.*

But when Topside rounded the next bend in the trail, the smile froze on her face. Instead of Rachel Hart or May Grover, Lisa instantly recognized Alex riding toward her about sixty yards ahead. He was aboard Chippewa, his favorite mount. And right beside him on the trail was Talisman, one of Max's best horses—with Nicole Adams in the saddle!

Alex obviously didn't see Lisa. He was looking at Nicole, his hand position sloppy and his heels bouncing all over the place as he grinned at her unabashedly. Nicole's riding position was a lot better, but she, too, was focusing more on her riding partner than on her horse. Lisa watched as the other girl fluttered her long, dark eyelashes at Alex.

Wow, Lisa thought, her mind strangely detached from the disturbing scene, *I didn't know people actually did that in real life.*

She wasn't sure what to do. Alex and Nicole—riding together? It had to be a date. Understanding hit her all at once, her mind spinning and the breath leaving her body as suddenly as if Topside had just given her a swift kick in the gut. Alex was out on a date with someone else.

151

It hasn't even been a week, she thought in stunned disbelief. *And here he is, already having a grand old time with another girl. Isn't he as torn up about our breakup as I am? Doesn't he care? Can he really like hanging out with someone like her?*

The thoughts and emotions passed through her in a matter of seconds, only long enough for Topside to take another few steps forward. When his hoof landed on a twig, it snapped it loudly. That was when Alex finally glanced forward and spotted Lisa. The smile froze on his face, and his grip on the reins tightened so suddenly that Chip tossed his head in annoyance.

Lisa held his gaze for a long moment as their horses continued toward each other, oblivious to their riders' distress. It was the most awkward moment Lisa could imagine, and she wasn't sure what to do.

I could start yelling and screaming about how he's cheating on me, even though he's really not, she thought. *Or I could burst into tears and make a big fool of myself that way. That would be productive. Or . . . Or I could try to be an adult about this.*

The last option seemed impossible at first. How could she just accept this and act like it was no big deal? This was *Alex*—the guy who had brought her back to life after her parents' divorce, the friend and confidant who'd listened to all her hopes and dreams and fears ever since. How could she be mature about the realization that she wasn't his whole world anymore, that he could just go out and find someone else after only a few days apart?

But as her horse approached the others with his ears pricked forward curiously, she knew she had to try. With great effort, she forced a pleasant smile onto her face. "Hi, Alex," she said. "Hi, Nicole. How's it going?" Her lips felt so numb and stiff that she was afraid her words would be unintelligible, but to her surprise her voice sounded almost normal.

Alex looked a little surprised, too. But he nodded. "Hey, Lisa," he said, so softly that the words were almost lost in the sound of the leaves rustling beneath the horses' feet.

"What's up?" Nicole added politely.

Lisa glanced over at her. She had hardly been aware of the other girl since first spotting the couple, but now she saw that Nicole obviously didn't share Alex's discomfort with the situation. She gazed directly at Lisa with a curious little half smile on her face. Her pretty, pretty face . . .

Shuddering slightly, Lisa turned away. She didn't want to get into any of that. This wasn't about Nicole, not really. It was about her and Alex.

She carefully maintained her calm expression until they had passed each other, Nicole steering Talisman behind Chip to make room on the trail. For a few minutes after that, Lisa kept Topside at a steady walk, willing herself not to glance back over her shoulder.

Finally she rounded another steep curve in the trail, guaranteeing that the others would be out of sight. Pulling Topside to a stop, she felt her posture crumble as she slumped over in the saddle, her whole body shaking. Topside shifted his feet nervously for a moment, but then he seemed to realize that they were taking a break and he lowered his head, snuffling around at the edges of the trail for any remaining greenery.

Lisa was hardly aware of what her horse was doing. She was busy replaying the meeting with Alex and Nicole in her head. It was unreal. How could someone like Alex, someone she'd thought she knew as well as she knew herself, move on so quickly, as if they'd never been in love at all?

She had no idea. But as upset as she was, somehow she didn't quite feel ready to head home and join her mother on the couch, drowning her sorrows in cookies and old movies.

No way, she thought, gathering her reins and sitting a little straighter in the saddle as she prepared to ride on. *I'm not Mom. I'm not going to fall apart because of this. If Alex can move on, so can I.*

EIGHT

It was so warm in her algebra classroom that Carole was having trouble staying awake, let alone focusing on polynomial equations or whatever it was that Mr. Whiteside was droning on and on about. Stifling a yawn, she shifted in her seat and drifted back into the daydream she'd been having, off and on, in almost every class so far that day.

"Carole, my darling wife and partner," Cam said gallantly. *"I'm so proud of you for winning that Olympic gold medal with the U.S. Equestrian Team last week. But are you sure you have the energy to finish training that promising dressage horse and then acting as Master of the Hunt for our foxhunting club?"*

"Absolutely," Carole replied, straightening the collar of her custom-made shadbelly coat. *"Your love gives me all the energy I need. Now if you'll excuse me, darling, I'd better go teach that beginners' riding class."*

Cam took her hand, gently peeled back the expensive deerskin glove covering it, and kissed the palm. "Of course, darling. Meanwhile, I'll go get started training those polo ponies our clients dropped off yesterday."

Then Carole walked out of their three-room office suite into the wide, clean-swept aisle of their two-hundred-stall stable, lit by large skylights overhead. As she walked toward the stadium-sized, heated indoor ring, she passed the flawlessly organized, well-appointed tack room, the warehouse-like feed room, and the roomy, cement-floored wash stall. Pausing just long enough to pat Starlight on the nose as he lounged in his sixteen-by-sixteen box stall, eating hay gathered from the lush fields surrounding Cam 'N Carole Stables by their full-time staff of fifty people, she then continued on to the ring to greet her adoring students. "Ms. Hanson! Ms. Hanson!" they cried eagerly. Carole was just trying to remember why she'd decided not to take Cam's name when they got married when—

"Ms. Hanson!" Mr. Whiteside's pale, bespectacled face frowned down at her with obvious annoyance. "Are you going to answer the question, or just sit there gaping like a fish?"

Carole gulped and sat up straight in her chair, trying to ignore the titters erupting all around as her classmates stared at her with amusement. *Yikes,* she thought sheepishly. *I guess I slipped a little farther into that daydream than I realized.*

"Um—I'm sorry," she stammered, deciding that honesty was the best policy. Well, partial honesty, at least. "I'm not sure about that answer."

Mr. Whiteside frowned, but nodded and moved on, stepping across the aisle and glancing down at the guy sitting there. "All right then," he said. "Mr. Levine, what about you? Do you have an answer?"

Whew! Carole thought. *That was close. I'd better watch it from now on, and pay more attention in class. In all my classes. Otherwise I'll be right back where I started again with my grades. And I definitely don't want that. Especially now.*

Unbidden, the image of Cam's smiling face floated into her mind. Not the way he'd appeared in her daydream, but the way he'd looked in real life as he'd fed her a strawberry and then leaned forward to kiss the juice off her lips.

Who needs crazy fantasy daydreams, anyway? Carole thought contentedly. *These days my real life's seeming a lot like some kind of amazing fantasy just the way it is.*

Realizing that she was slipping away again into her own head, she quickly picked up her pencil and blinked at Mr. Whiteside, who was at the board scribbling equations. She knew that Cam would want her to do well in school. He wanted her to do whatever she needed to do to be able to go back to riding full-time again. Not to mention being able to date full-time . . .

That's why he put Starlight away for me after our ride, Carole thought, feeling her cheeks go pink. *He didn't want me to get in trouble, because if I did, Dad might not let me go out with him again. And he's right—I've got to shape up and keep my grades and stuff under control. My whole social life is at stake now, not just my time at Pine Hollow.*

She did her best to stop thinking about Cam and focus on her teacher, who was talking about variables, as far as Carole could tell. But it wasn't long before her mind started to wander again. She couldn't seem to stop thinking about Cam and the way he made her feel. Special. Appreciated. Beautiful. Being with him was so easy, so natural and right, with no confusion or awkwardness or constant wondering about what the other person was thinking . . .

For a split second, Ben Marlow's face swam into her consciousness. But she shook her head quickly, not wanting to get all muddled up and anxious as she always did when she started thinking about Ben.

It was much easier to just lean back in her seat and return her thoughts to Cam. After all, she needed to remember all the wonderful things he'd said to her the previous day so that she could report them to Stevie and Lisa later. And then of course there was the big decision about what to wear for their date to the CARL party on Friday . . .

"Gesundheit," the town records clerk said, glancing at Stevie over the tops of her bifocals.

"Thanks." Stevie sniffled and wiped her nose with a crumpled tissue she found in her pocket, then smiled apologetically at the clerk, hoping that the woman would at least appreciate the fact that Stevie hadn't blown her nose on the stack of boring old zoning permits and yellowed deeds stacked in front of her. "I guess I'm allergic to dust."

The woman went back to her work, and Stevie looked down at her pile of musty papers and sighed. She'd been buried in deadly dull research ever since school had let out half an hour earlier, and she decided it was time for a break.

If I don't get out of here soon, I'll go completely insane, she thought grimly. *And that won't reflect very well on the vaunted history of dear old Fenton Hall, will it? Besides, if they lock me in the loony bin, Cassidy would probably just figure I had even more time on my hands, and she'd come by to drop off a few old Willow Creek phone books or twenty-year-old attendance reports for me to read.*

Her mind made up, she stacked the materials she'd used and returned them to the clerk, promising to return on another day to finish looking through them. She was tempted to race for the door like a stall-sour horse heading for pasture, but she forced herself to maintain a sedate walk until she got outside.

She had to pause and blink a few times to allow her eyes to adjust to the bright yellow-orange glare of the afternoon sun after the dim, dusty overheads inside. Then she glanced at her watch. She had promised to meet Cassidy back at school as soon as she finished at the records office, but she couldn't quite bring herself to return just yet.

"Everybody needs food for thought, right?" she muttered, staring at the doughnut shop across the street. Then she had a better idea. "Pizza!" she exclaimed, her stomach letting out a hopeful grumble.

Checking her watch again, she decided she had time for a quick slice before returning to her drudgery. There was a pizza place across the street from Fenton Hall, so technically it was right on her way. Cassidy couldn't possibly object to that, could she?

It didn't take much for Stevie to convince herself. She headed down the street at a rapid walk, her mouth already watering at the thought of a thick, gooey slice of extra-cheese-and-mushrooms, fresh from Giordanos' authentic stone pizza oven.

Less than ten minutes later, she was pushing open the door of Giordano's Authentic Pizza and Pasta. Inhaling deeply as the aroma of garlic and oregano surrounded her like a warm cloud, Stevie stepped inside. Giordano's was one of two popular pizza restaurants in Willow Creek, and the one Stevie preferred for a couple of reasons. First of all, its location made it extremely convenient for after-school pit stops—especially on days when the Fenton Hall cafeteria was serving its infamous Mystery Stew—the one that made students double-check the whereabouts of the janitor's dog. Second, Stevie had spent a couple of months the previous summer working at the other place, Pizza Manor, and visiting there now always made her feel strangely anxious, as if the manager, Mr. Andrews, was going to yell at her for sitting around stuffing her face instead of working.

The sign at the hostess's stand read Please Seat Yourself, so Stevie stepped farther in and glanced around for an empty table. As her gaze swept past a row of cozy, candlelit booths, she did a double take. Her twin brother was sitting there holding up a large slice of cheese pizza. But that wasn't the strange part. The strange part was that Nicole Adams was leaning forward to take a bite, giggling as the stringy cheese dripped down her chin. She and Alex were both squeezed into the same side of the booth, despite the fact that there was nobody at all sitting on the opposite side of the table.

Stevie just stared blankly for a moment, not really comprehending what she was seeing. *What are they doing?* she wondered. *Why are they sitting like that?*

Then Alex picked up a napkin and carefully wiped the cheese off Nicole's chin, and Stevie snapped out of it. Fury shot through her body as she remembered Alex's late return the previous Saturday night. Now that she thought about it, she hadn't seen much of her brother that whole week. Had he been spending even more time with Nicole than she had realized?

There was only one way to find out. *One date is one thing—that would just be following the rules,* she thought grimly, already racing toward the booth. *But this is too much!*

Alex glanced up in surprise as Stevie skidded to a stop at the end of the table. "Oh!" he said. "Stevie. I was hoping you were the waitress bringing our refills." He gestured toward his empty soda glass.

Stevie hardly heard him. "What do you think you're doing!" she exclaimed hotly. "How can you do this to Lisa, you jerk? How do you think she would feel if she saw you here with . . . with . . ." She glanced at Nicole with utter disdain.

Alex looked startled for a second, then his expression darkened into annoyance and then anger. "I don't know, Stevie," he said coldly. "But in any case, it would be none of your business. So why don't you go take a flying leap?"

"Fine." Stevie tossed her head, too aggravated to come up with a decent retort. "You're right. If you want to ruin your own life, it's your business. Just don't ask me to plead your desperate, pathetic case with Lisa when you realize your mistake." With that, she spun on her heel and stomped away.

She'd completely lost her appetite, so she didn't stop until she'd burst out the door onto the sidewalk. She stopped and hovered uncertainly for a moment—she was far too worked up to return to Fenton Hall but not sure where else she should go. It was too cold to just stand around thinking about it, so she started to walk, wandering aimlessly past the shops and offices on Convent Street without really seeing anything except the image of Alex and Nicole together.

After a moment, the chilly December weather helped to cool Stevie's temper as well as her hot, flushed face. Before she'd gone half a block, she was starting to realize that she might have been a little out of line. *I guess maybe Alex was right to be mad*, she thought with a shrug. *It really is none of my business who he wants to go out with. It's just that I don't want to see Lisa get hurt . . .*

As she thought about that for a second, it occurred to her that she was forgetting one very important fact. The whole breakup thing had been Lisa's idea. True, Alex had been expressing a few doubts even before that, but he hadn't been the one who'd insisted on giving the relationship a rest. That was what Lisa had wanted. She had wanted them to see other people for a while to gain some perspective on what they had together.

Still, I doubt she expected Alex to start seeing some total bimbo like Nicole, Stevie thought with a slight frown. *Nicole's practically the polar opposite of Lisa. Lisa is smart, Nicole's an airhead. Lisa is pretty in a classy, elegant way, while Nicole has to rely on tons of hair bleach and makeup and a push-up bra to get guys to notice her. Lisa really cares about Alex, and Nicole is probably just in it for laughs.*

Stevie paused at the corner, glancing both ways

before heading across. As she stepped up on the opposite curb, she shoved her hands into her jacket pockets for warmth.

Okay, okay, she admitted reluctantly, feeling sheepish, *I guess it's not up to me to decide who Alex should date. He's a big boy, and he can make his own decisions. Even if they are incredibly stupid.*

She bit her lip, knowing what she had to do. Even if the thought of Alex dating Nicole turned her stomach, Stevie had to apologize to her brother for butting in and making a scene. Of course, that didn't mean she was eager to rush back to Giordano's and beg his forgiveness right then and there.

I'll give him a few hours to cool off, she decided. *Maybe I can catch him at home before dinner. In any case, I'll definitely make things right sometime tonight.* She felt a little better as soon as she'd reached that decision.

But only for a second. That was how long it took her to remember that there was one more person involved in the whole situation. Lisa. Should Stevie tell her what she'd seen or not? Lisa was her best friend. How could she keep something like that from her? Then again, maybe it would only make Lisa feel worse. Would Stevie be a better friend by filling her in or by keeping quiet?

She wasn't sure what the answer was. But thinking about it made her think about another confused friendship. There was one way that Stevie definitely was *not* being a good friend these days. That was by letting Scott continue under the impression that he had any chance at all with her.

I've been putting it off too long, but I've got to talk to him, she told herself. *I have to be honest with him— tell him that I'm crazy about him as a friend, but my heart belongs to Phil. Scott will have to accept that if he wants our friendship to continue.*

She bit her lip again, dreading the whole conversation. But as much as she would have loved to avoid it, she knew she couldn't. If she wanted to be a good friend to Scott, it was something she simply had to do—and soon.

Turning around, she started walking briskly back toward Fenton Hall, figuring that she'd wasted enough time avoiding her duty. And she wasn't only thinking about Cassidy.

Scott will just have to find a way to deal, she thought. *All I can do is try to break it to him gently.*

NINE

"Tanner Finnegan's kind of cute," Lisa murmured into the gray mare's ear, switching her body brush to the other hand. "But I don't know if I could deal with his constant wisecracking on a date. Then there's Gary Korman—he's always seemed like a really nice guy, even if he's not my usual type. But I'm pretty sure he has a crush on that new girl in our physics class. Then there's that Fenton Hall guy I met at Stevie's party. What was his name again? Kevin, Ken . . . ?" She trailed off with a sigh.

What am I doing? she wondered, giving Eve a pat and then bending down to exchange the body brush for a grooming cloth. *I'm standing here talking to a horse about which guys I should date. Of course, the way I'm feeling, Eve just might have a better handle on that particular topic than I do.*

Smiling at the image that popped into her head— herself lying on a psychiatrist's couch while Eve sat in a chair tapping her chin thoughtfully with one hoof as she gave advice—Lisa got back to work on her

166

grooming. She'd just returned from taking a quick ride in the schooling ring; she hadn't quite worked up the nerve to go back out on the trails after what had happened the day before.

Now she was trying to psych herself up to ask someone out. But so far she wasn't having much success. "I don't have to be madly in love with someone to invite him out for a burger, right?" Lisa asked Eve as she polished the mare's coat to a sheen. "I just have to start somewhere. Get right back on the horse, so to speak."

She was still smiling at her own bad joke when she heard footsteps approaching. Glancing over her shoulder, she spotted Scott and Callie. "Hey, Lisa!" Scott called. "How's it going?"

"Fine," Lisa said. "What are you guys up to?"

"I have an appointment to see a couple of horses at a farm over toward Quantico," Callie replied.

"And as usual, I'm playing chauffeur." Scott smiled. Then he cocked his head to one side and studied Lisa's face. "Hey, are you okay? You look kind of glum."

Lisa shrugged, not wanting to get into it. "I'm just at loose ends, I guess," she said lightly.

"Why don't you come with us?" Scott suggested. "There's always room in the car for one more. Not much room, but hey, you don't take up that much space, right?" He grinned. People were always giving him a hard time about the tiny, cramped backseat of his sporty little car.

Lisa hesitated. It was tempting to accept his offer, just for the sake of having something social to do. "Are you sure I won't be in the way?"

"Of course not," Callie replied with a smile. "You can back me up when I refuse to buy whatever they show me today. They're supposed to be some pretty nice Arabians, but the way my luck's been going, they'll probably be Percherons. Or maybe goats."

Lisa laughed. "Okay," she said. "In that case, it's a deal. Just let me finish up here—it should only take a minute."

Soon Eve's grooming was complete and the three of them piled into Scott's car. At the end of Pine Hollow's gravel driveway, Scott turned left, heading for the highway. During the drive, the conversation centered around Callie's horse search. Lisa didn't know a whole lot about long-distance riding—she'd gone on one endurance ride when she was younger, but she still had lots of questions for Callie about what kind of horse she wanted and what her plans were once she found the right one.

When they arrived at the stable, Scott parked the car while Lisa and Callie went to meet the owner, who was waiting for them in front of the main build-ing. The place was a fairly large facility specializing in Arabians, and the owner had three endurance prospects to show Callie. As Scott joined the two girls at the fence of a roomy paddock, the stable owner led out a stunning dapple gray gelding with a dark mane and an alert expression. "Nice," Callie said, looking at the horse appraisingly.

Lisa was inclined to agree with that sentiment. She had seen a lot of expensive horseflesh in her day—Topside, for instance, had been a champion show jumper before his owner had retired him, and the Thoroughbred mare Calypso had been a star of the racetrack before coming to live at Pine Hollow.

But it's not like I would ever consider owning a super-fancy horse like that myself, Lisa thought, shooting Callie a glance out of the corner of her eye as the stable owner began explaining the horse's finer points. *I can't believe Callie's looking at this kind of quality. I mean, I knew she was serious about endurance riding, but this . . .*

"Nothing but the best for my sister," Scott said lightly, leaning on the fence beside Lisa as Callie let herself into the paddock and walked over to examine the beautiful gelding.

Lisa blinked at him in surprise, wondering if he'd read her mind. "I was just thinking how incredible he looks," she said carefully, nodding toward the horse. The last thing she wanted to do was embarrass Scott by pointing out how lucky his family was to have enough money to afford such a horse.

Scott didn't embarrass easily, though. He just laughed. "Okay, you know how Callie and I like to complain about having a famous father with a high-profile job? Well, I guess you could say that this is the upside." He grinned and winked.

Lisa laughed, reminded once again of why everyone liked Scott so much. It was no wonder he'd fit so easily into their little group of friends right from the beginning. Even though he'd only been around for six months or so, Lisa already had a hard time remembering life without him.

The two of them turned to watch as the stable owner led the gelding around the ring a few times so that Callie could see how he moved. "Looks like he has a nice smooth trot, and he seems spirited but eager to please," Lisa commented, wondering why shopping for a date couldn't be more like shopping for a horse. At least then she'd have some idea what she was doing.

Scott gave her a searching look. "You still seem kind of down," he said abruptly. "Are you ever going to tell me what's wrong?"

Lisa was so startled by the question that she just shrugged in reply. "It's nothing."

"It doesn't look like nothing."

Biting her lip, Lisa shrugged again. "No, really," she insisted. "It's no big deal. I'm just in kind of a weird mood today, that's all."

"Come on," Scott wheedled. "It's me. Your friend."

All of a sudden she gave in. Why not tell him what she was thinking about? Maybe it would help to get a guy's perspective on her situation. "Okay." She took a deep breath and shot him a quick glance before returning her gaze to the horse in the paddock. "I'm sure you've heard that Alex and I—um, well, we're supposed to see other people. For a while. I, um, I know that Alex is already going ahead with that. And I want to get moving, too. It's just that it's been so long since I had to think about this sort of thing. I—I guess I'm having some trouble getting back in the swing of things." She laughed self-consciously, remembering her earlier "conversation" with Eve. "I can't even figure out who I might like to go out with."

"I see." Scott rubbed his chin thoughtfully, his blue eyes serious as they gazed out toward Callie and the Arabian. "Well, it's totally understandable that you'd be feeling that way right now. You and Alex were together a long time, and it's got to be tough to even think about getting to know someone else right now. Especially since you haven't had all that long to adjust yet."

"Right," Lisa said, grateful for his understanding words, which mirrored what she'd been thinking all day.

She was suddenly very glad that she'd decided to confide in Scott. It felt good to talk things out with someone who could actually talk back. *Besides, Scott's amazingly easy to talk to,* she thought, turning to look at him appreciatively. His profile as he watched the action in the paddock was strong and handsome. Remembering Stevie's dilemma, Lisa smiled slightly. *You know, if Stevie didn't already have a great guy like Phil, she could certainly do worse than Scott. A lot worse.*

"I've got only one thing to suggest." Scott suddenly turned his head to look at her. "Would you like to go to the CARL party on Friday?"

Lisa was a little flustered that he'd caught her staring at him. "Um, yeah," she said distractedly, quickly shifting her gaze back to Callie and the horse. "I am going to that."

"No." Scott chuckled. "I'm sorry, my bad. What I should have said is, Lisa, would you please do me the honor of coming to the CARL party on Friday with me?"

Lisa's jaw dropped. Scott was asking her out on a *date*? She must have sounded even more pathetic than she'd realized. "It's okay," she said quickly. "I really don't mind just hanging out with the group at the CARL thing." She laughed self-consciously again. "I appreciate the offer, but I wasn't fishing for a pity date or anything."

"No need to turn me down on that account." Scott was gazing at her steadily. "It definitely wouldn't be a pity date."

"What do you mean?" Lisa asked cautiously.

Scott cleared his throat. "I mean, I've been thinking about asking you out ever since I heard that you and Alex had broken up." He had been leaning on the paddock fence as they talked, but now he stood up straight as he turned to her. "I've thought you were one of the most beautiful girls I'd ever met since the first time I laid eyes on you. And once I got to know you better, I realized you're one of the smartest, nicest, and most special people I've ever met, too."

Lisa was having a hard time taking in what was happening. Gripping the top rail of the fence with one hand, she stared up at his earnest face in total amazement. "You—You really, um . . ." She trailed off, not even sure how to respond to what he was saying.

Scott smiled. "I realize this must be coming as kind of a surprise," he said matter-of-factly. "I mean, I've had a major crush on you for a while now. But I've been doing my best to keep it to myself." He shrugged and shoved his hands into his jeans pockets. "Alex is a friend. And I respected your relationship with him too much to want to mess with it. But now that you're thinking about dating again, and the field seems to be wide open . . . well, I guess it seemed like the moment to take a shot. So how about it? Will you let me take you out on Friday and try to show you a good time?"

Lisa was completely blown away. Scott Forester had a crush on *her*? *But he's, like, Mr. Popular,* she thought in stunned disbelief. *Practically every girl that meets him wants to jump his bones. Even*

Veronica diAngelo, the man magnet, just about threw herself at him.

Realizing that Scott was waiting for an answer, Lisa gulped. What should she do? Scott was her friend. She didn't want to risk that friendship just to have a date for Friday night. Not to mention that it seemed kind of weird to go out with someone who knew Alex so well . . .

"Okay," she blurted out before she quite realized what she was doing. "I'd love to go. It's a date."

"Great!" Scott looked genuinely happy. "If you don't have your ticket yet, I'll pick up a pair for us tomorrow."

Lisa nodded in agreement, trying to look as pleased about their plans as he did, but inside she wasn't sure she was doing the right thing. She was relieved when Scott turned the conversation back to Callie, who was helping the stable owner put a saddle on the gray horse. Watching his sister carefully, Scott started chatting about her reactions to the other horses she'd seen so far.

Lisa did her best to nod and smile in all the right places as Scott talked, but her mind was still trying to wrap itself around the concept that he wanted to date her. *I never in a million years would have suspected that he was interested in me,* she thought. *I never would have guessed that I was the reason he was hanging around Pine Hollow so much. That I was the one he—Yikes!*

She'd just realized something. If what Scott had just told her was true, that meant that Lisa really was the only girl at Pine Hollow who'd been occupying his thoughts lately.

Lisa gulped. *Okay, I know Stevie is in love with Phil—she definitely doesn't want to go out with Scott,* she thought. *But that doesn't mean it won't sting a little when she finds out he doesn't have some mad crush on her like she thought he did. Stevie's ego is pretty healthy, but still . . .* Lisa sighed softly, leaning forward on the paddock fence as she imagined her friend's reaction. *I guess I'll just have to break it to her gently.*

As Stevie walked into her English lit classroom the next day, she was still thinking about her dilemma. How could she tell Scott they were never going to be a couple without totally blowing him away and ruining their friendship?

Ignoring the chaos around her as her classmates laughed and chattered and goofed off, Stevie sat down at her desk and pulled out her textbook. Staring into space, she tried to figure out what to say.

Okay. Maybe I should just be straight and matter-of-fact about it, she thought. *I can just march right up to him and say, "Listen here, Scott. I know you want me, but you've got to get over it. My heart belongs to Phil and that's that." And then he'd say, "Thank you for your honesty, my darling Stevie. But I just can't live without* having you all to myself. So if you'll excuse me, I'd better go kill myself now."

Stevie shook her head and wrinkled her nose. That wasn't likely to happen. But she still wasn't sure the blunt and up-front approach was the way to go. She wanted to let him down easy, not blow him away.

I've got to be careful. If he's too hurt and embarrassed, it could totally ruin our friendship, she reminded herself as her teacher rapped her wooden pointer on the blackboard for attention. *No, I'd better be more tactful. Find the right words to soften the blow. Something kind and maybe poetic.*

She glanced at the textbook on the desk in front of her. Flipping idly through its pages as the teacher began to lecture, Stevie hoped for inspiration. But all she seemed to find were lovey-dovey passages from poets mooning over lost loves.

Stevie sighed and turned back to the chapter her teacher was discussing. *I'm supposed to be a writer now, right?* she told herself, thinking of the nice things Theresa had said about her first article. *I should be able to come up with something to say to him.*

But by the time the class ended forty minutes later, she still hadn't come up with a thing. Gathering up her books and shoving them back into her pack, she left the room and headed toward her locker. Lunch period was next. That would give her the perfect opportunity to get some advice from Callie.

Stevie was digging in the bottom of her locker for

her lunch, which had somehow become wedged beneath her spare pair of riding boots and the plastic bag containing her dirty towel from phys ed, when she heard a shrill scream of laughter from somewhere nearby. Familiar laughter.

Stevie frowned and glanced over her shoulder. Sure enough, Veronica was walking down the hall in her direction, a small notebook in her hand and a pencil tucked into the sleek dark hair behind one ear. She was using another pencil to scribble busily in the notebook. Stevie's gaze shifted to Nicole Adams, who was walking along beside Veronica, chatting rapidly and waving her hands around. For some reason, the scene made Stevie feel uneasy. Were the two of them just trading makeup tips or debating which member of the basketball team was the best kisser, as usual? Stevie certainly hoped so. Because if Veronica was serious about that gossip-column thing . . .

Just then Veronica glanced her way. When she saw that Stevie was watching her, she smirked very unsettlingly before turning back to Nicole.

Stevie shook her head. She had more important things to worry about than what was going on inside Veronica's devious little mind. It wasn't like Theresa was going to allow Veronica to print all sorts of horrible lies about Stevie in her column.

As soon as that thought occurred to her, Stevie felt better. *I know exactly what's going to happen,* she thought, finally extricating her lunch and slamming her locker door shut. *Veronica will turn in some poisonous, totally slanderous piece of garbage for her first column. Then Theresa will realize what kind of nonjournalist loser she's dealing with, and she'll tell Veronica to take a hike and stay away from her paper. So why worry about it?*

Callie was saving her a seat at a table at the far end of the cafeteria. Sliding into it, Stevie plopped her lunch bag down and glanced at the magazine that was lying open on the table beside Callie's tuna sandwich. The spread in view showed a compact chestnut gelding climbing a steep incline, every muscle gleaming in the hot sun as his rider leaned forward over his sweaty neck.

"Wow," Stevie commented. "Nice-looking horse."

"Tell me about it." Callie sighed and flipped the magazine shut. "He and his owner won the Tevis Cup last year. He's awesome. I just wish I could snap my fingers and clone him so I'd have a decent horse to ride."

"Does that mean your farm visit yesterday didn't go well?" Stevie asked.

Callie shrugged and picked up her sandwich, gazing at it blankly. "No, actually I finally saw some good ones yesterday," she admitted. "Three Arabs. One of them had some dicey hooves, but the other two seemed promising." She bit her lip and lowered her sandwich to the table without taking a bite. "I just wish it was easier to know what kind of horse would be best for me—and to recognize it when I see it."

Stevie raised one eyebrow in surprise. "Do mine ears deceive me?" she commented. "Since when is the famous Callie Forester scared of a challenge?"

Callie smiled weakly. "I know, I know," she said. "This should be the fun part. It's just that the stakes are so high—I don't want to make a mistake."

"I hear that." Stevie cleared her throat as she opened her bag and pulled out an orange, a cold chicken leg, and one of her favorite treats, a SuperCrunch granola bar. Meanwhile her mind was already returning to her own problem. "Speaking of mistakes . . ."

Her voice trailed off as she happened to notice a certain well-dressed would-be gossip columnist heading their way. With a slight frown, she watched Veronica approach. *What does she want now?* she thought irritably. *If she doesn't stop getting in my face, I'm never going to have time to figure out how to deal with Scott.*

Veronica stopped at the next table over, and Stevie sighed in relief. She turned her attention back to Callie, who was flipping through her magazine. "Anyway," she began again, "I wanted to ask your advice about something."

"Sure," Callie said, picking up her carton of orange juice. "Just as long as it's not about what to wear to the CARL thing on Friday. I already spent half an hour discussing that particular topic with Scott this morning." She shrugged and smiled knowingly as she glanced at Stevie. "I think he's a little nervous about his big date with Lisa."

"No, it's not that. I—" Stevie froze. "What did you just say?"

Callie lowered her juice and wiped her mouth with her napkin. "Which part?" she asked. "You mean about what to wear?"

"No, no." Stevie waved her hands frantically. "The part about Scott."

"You mean his date with Lisa?" Callie shrugged. "What about it? Didn't she fill you in?" Her expression suddenly cleared. "Oh! Don't tell me you didn't know?"

Stevie grinned weakly. "Okay. I won't tell you." She shook her head, trying to loosen the confusion that was reigning inside her brain. "So let me get this straight. Scott—your brother—is going to the CARL party with Lisa? As in Lisa Atwood?"

"Uh-huh. He asked her yesterday afternoon." Callie pursed her lips, watching Stevie carefully. "As it turns out, he's had, um, a little crush on her for a while now. He just never let on until yesterday."

"Oh." Stevie sat there for a moment, trying to take it all in. She wasn't sure whether to feel surprised, relieved, skeptical, or humiliated. At the moment all those emotions were mixed up at once, fighting for prominence. "So all this time that I thought—"

"Yep." Callie smiled sympathetically. "But don't feel bad. You practically had me convinced that he was into you, too."

Stevie grimaced. That didn't make her feel much better. *How could I have been so wrong?* she thought. *And more importantly, how could I have told everybody I know all about it?*

Before she could think much more about that, she noticed that Veronica was on the move once again. This time, she sauntered straight up to Stevie and Callie and stopped, staring at them with her arms crossed over the front of her expensive cashmere twinset and a wicked smile on her face. "Hello, girls," she drawled. "What's going on? What's the gossip here at the loser end of the caf?"

Callie just rolled her eyes and returned her attention to her magazine. But Stevie was already off balance from Callie's news, and she was in no mood to put up with anything from Veronica. "If you want to know what's going on with losers, just go take a look in the mirror," she snapped. "That's your favorite way to pass the time anyway, isn't it?"

Veronica snorted. "Very mature, Stevie," she said coolly. "But never mind. I already have all the info I need—you'll see that for yourself when the paper comes out on Friday."

Stevie gritted her teeth, willing herself to just let it drop. Veronica was only trying to get a rise out of her. Why give her the satisfaction?

The two of them glared at each other silently. The tense moment was shattered a few seconds later when George Wheeler bustled up to the table.

"Hi!" George said cheerfully, his gaze focused on Callie and a broad smile on his face. Scooting past Veronica, who was staring at him as if he were a particularly ripe bit of manure smeared on the toe of her custom-made boot, he plopped down in the empty seat beside Callie. "What are you eating there, Callie? It looks good."

Veronica rolled her eyes and walked away, muttering about losers. Stevie let out a long breath, grateful for once for George's general cluelessness. As he started chattering eagerly about some Web site he'd just found about endurance riding, Stevie quickly stuffed her lunch back in the bag. Now that she didn't have to worry about talking to Scott anymore, she figured it wouldn't hurt to hit the library and get a jump on her next round of boring research. While she was at it, maybe she could get a grip on the news about Scott and Lisa—at the moment she was still reeling from the idea that she'd been totally wrong about his feelings toward her. But in the back of her mind, she was already starting to wonder what this turn of events might mean for Lisa and Alex.

Standing up, she gave Callie a little wave to indicate that she was leaving. Callie returned the wave weakly, while George still seemed completely oblivious to Stevie's existence on the planet. Stevie felt a little guilty about abandoning Callie to him, but she figured her friend could handle it. If Callie didn't want George hanging around, she would tell him so.

Meanwhile, I'd better go bury myself in dusty old yearbooks, Stevie thought as she hurried toward the exit. *And when I come up for air, maybe I'll be ready to look Scott in the face without feeling like the world's biggest idiot.*

She winced, imagining exactly how hard Scott would laugh if he knew what she'd thought. She could only hope that neither Callie nor Lisa ever, ever, ever told him. Or Carole. Or Alex. Or Phil. Or—

Yikes, Stevie thought sheepishly, stopping in the middle of the hallway as she realized just how many people she'd let in on her "secret" theory. *I guess maybe this is why some people seem to think I have a big mouth!*

TEN

10

"And forget about ever making plans more than two days ahead of time," Mrs. Atwood said bitterly, stirring a packet of sugar-free sweetener into her tea as she stood at the kitchen counter. "It's all part of their fear of commitment."

Lisa glanced up from examining her fingernails. She was sitting at the kitchen table, where she'd been trapped, ever since arriving home from school fifteen minutes earlier, by her mother's complaining about men.

"That may be true of some guys," she said.

Her mother snorted. "Forget some, dear. They're *all* like that. You might as well get it through your head now that you can't count on a man for anything. Not when the chips are down. If you understand that, it'll save you a lot of heartache in the long run."

Under the guise of stretching, Lisa sneaked a glance at the clock on the wall over the refrigerator. Miraculously, her mother had actually stated her intention to go into work that evening, and Lisa was counting the seconds until she had the house to herself. *At least I actually have someplace to go tomorrow night,* she thought, automatically feigning a sympathetic smile as her mother rambled on about the evil ways of all men. *Thank goodness. Friday and Saturday nights are always the roughest for Mom. And that makes them rougher for anyone who has to listen to her.* She felt guilty for the thought, but shrugged it off. *Let Aunt Marianne take her turn for a while. After the week I've had, I need to have fun for one night at least.*

Thinking about her plans for the following evening made Lisa feel a little jumpy. She still wasn't sure what to make of some of the things Scott had said to her the previous afternoon. But she'd decided that the best way to proceed was to act as if their "date" was just a friendly evening outing. That was probably how Scott was looking at it, too.

". . . and of course, they all only want one thing from a woman," Mrs. Atwood said grimly, interrupting Lisa's train of thought. "You're not too young to start realizing that, Lisa."

Lisa gulped, wishing she could be anyplace else in the world right then. Her mother was staring at her, seeming to expect some kind of response. "Um . . ." Lisa began helplessly.

At that moment the phone rang shrilly. Lisa jumped, then smiled with relief as she got up and hurried over to answer it.

"Hello, Atwood residence," she said politely.

"Hi, is this Lisa?" a familiar voice said. "It's Scott."

"Oh! Hi. Could you hold on a sec?" Lisa covered the mouthpiece with her hand and glanced at her mother. "It's for me. Uh, a friend from Pine Hollow."

Her mother nodded but didn't seem inclined to leave the room. Fortunately the phone was a cordless model, so Lisa quickly stepped out into the hall. Then she removed her hand.

"Hi, Scott?" she said. "Sorry about that."

"I hope I didn't catch you at a bad time," Scott said. "I was just calling to arrange a time for tomorrow night. The fund-raiser starts at seven, so I thought I'd come by and pick you up at about ten of if that's okay with you."

"Sure, that sounds fine."

"Great." Scott's voice was warm and friendly. "I'm really looking forward to it."

Lisa gulped. "Uh, me too." Was it her imagination, or was this date starting to feel a lot more like a romantic deal than a friendly one? She couldn't quite put her finger on it, but there was something about the way that Scott had called her, and the formality of his invitation, that made her think of an old-fashioned word that her grandmother had liked to use. *Wooing,* she thought. *That's what it sort of feels like. Scott's wooing me.*

The idea made her more than a little uncomfortable. She wasn't sure she particularly wanted to be wooed, by Scott or anyone else. It was too soon. She and Alex had been broken up for only a few days.

And we aren't even officially, permanently broken up, not really, she thought, clutching the phone as Scott said something about picking up their tickets. *We're just taking a break until the end of the month, figuring out where things stand.*

But as the image of Alex and Nicole riding through the woods flashed through her mind—the two of them laughing and flirting and looking for all the world like a happy couple—she couldn't quite believe that things were really that simple. She had no idea what was going to happen at the end of the month. But until things were settled between her and Alex, she didn't want to get too involved with anyone. She just hoped Scott would understand that.

". . . anyway, I'd better run," he was saying at the other end of the line. "It's my turn to set the table tonight. But I'll see you tomorrow night."

"See you then," Lisa agreed.

"Can't wait," Scott added. "Bye, Lisa."

"Bye."

Lisa hit the Off button on the phone and wandered back into the kitchen, wondering what she was getting herself into with this date. It hadn't really seemed like a big deal at first, but now . . .

"Oh, good, there you are." Her mother was seated at the table, sipping her tea. "I was waiting for you. I wanted to talk to you about something."

"What is it, Mom?" Lisa steeled herself for another lecture on how to spot a rotten man. Why hadn't she escaped upstairs to her room when she'd had the chance?

Her mother pushed her teacup aside. "I've been doing a lot of thinking since—well, lately." She frowned, and Lisa guessed that she was thinking about the latest man who'd done her wrong. "Anyway, I've realized it's time for me to take control of my own life. It's up to me to change it for the better."

Lisa blinked, startled. "You what?" Her mother had never been very good at admitting her mistakes or accepting responsibility for her own happiness. "Um, that's great, Mom."

Mrs. Atwood nodded firmly. "I hope you'll support me in this, Lisa," she said. "It's time for some major changes."

"Of course I support you, Mom," Lisa said quickly, hoping that her mother's solution to her problems involved more than a new wardrobe or a trip to some fancy, expensive spa. "Uh, what sorts of changes did you have in mind?"

Her mother smiled. "I'm glad you're willing to go along with me on this, dear," she said. "Because it will affect you, too. You see, I realized that I really need to be around people who will support me."

For a moment Lisa thought her mother was referring to her. But her next words made her real meaning clear.

"I want to be closer to your aunt Marianne," Mrs. Atwood said calmly. "That's why I think we should move up to New Jersey. Right after the holidays."

When Stevie arrived at Pine Hollow that afternoon, she was looking forward to a quick ride on Belle. She had an hour and a half of free time before she was due to meet Cassidy at the office of *The Willow Creek Gazette,* the town newspaper. Cassidy had mentioned that they would need to go through fifty years' worth of back issues looking for articles about the school, so Stevie figured she'd better have some fun while she had the chance.

She was crossing the entryway, headed for the tack room to pick up Belle's tack, when Max burst out of his office. "Hi, Max," Stevie sang out.

Max stopped short and blinked at her, looking stressed. "What?" he demanded.

Stevie laughed. "Hi," she repeated. "It's a greeting. Perhaps you've heard of it?"

"I'm not in the mood, Stevie," Max snapped with a frown. "Now if you'll excuse me, I've got about a thousand things to do in the next two hours."

With a stab of guilt, Stevie realized that preparing for the Starlight Ride was probably right up there on Max's thousand-item to-do list. And that was at least partly because Stevie hadn't been living up to her promise to help out. In fact, she hadn't helped at all, let alone started gathering information for her story about the upcoming event.

"As a matter of fact, I was just going to volunteer my services," she told Max. "I'm here for Starlight Ride duty. So put me to work."

Max looked surprised, and Stevie would have sworn she saw a spark of gratitude in his tired-looking blue eyes. With a quick nod he did just as she suggested, assigning her to start by bringing down the torches from the storage area above the office wing. "And when you're done with that, you can start making calls to the landowners whose property we need to cross," he added, already turning to continue on his way. "There's a map and a phone list on the desk."

"You got it," Stevie said, calculating how long it would take her to finish with the torches. With any luck, she could finish up both tasks before she had to leave to meet Cassidy.

So much for my nice, relaxing, fun ride, she thought with a twinge of regret. *But Belle will just have to understand. I promised Max I'd help out, and I promised Theresa she'd have her article one week from today. And Stevie Lake never goes back on her word.*

Craig Skippack stepped back and cast a critical eye at the freshly painted walls of the CARL reception area. "Looks good," he announced. "I don't think we need to put another coat on after all."

Carole wiped her brow and exchanged smiles with a couple of her fellow volunteers. They'd worked hard on the painting, and Carole was glad it had paid off. "Great," she said. "So what should we do next?"

Craig glanced around the room. In addition to the clean, pale yellow walls, the reception area now sported sparkling-clean windows and a freshly mopped floor. "I think we're done in here," he said. "And the runs and the rest of the indoors look great." He shrugged and smiled, scratching his head through his thinning brown hair. "We're actually running ahead of schedule for a change."

"That's a first," one of the other volunteers joked.

Carole laughed along with the others. "What about the outside?" she asked. "Someone still has to rake down the paddock, and that hedge along the sidewalk out front could use some trimming, and—"

"Hey, who's in charge here, anyway?" Craig interrupted with a good-natured grin. "But you're right, Carole. There are still a few more things to take care of outside. But nothing too major. I thought we'd all be working straight through tomorrow afternoon, but . . ." He shrugged expressively. "Anyway, there's no sense in everyone hanging around. Why don't you guys head out?"

"Really?" Carole checked her watch. It was only

four-fifteen, and her father wasn't expecting her home until six-thirty. "You mean we can leave now?"

Craig smiled and nodded. "You're officially off the hook," he declared. "I'll see you all tomorrow night at the fund-raiser."

Carole and the others let out a ragged cheer. As the other volunteers started to chat about the next evening's party, Carole headed for the phone. Her heart was pounding loudly. She dialed her home number first. When the answering machine picked up, she left her father a quick message, saying that her volunteering had ended early and she was going over to Pine Hollow for a couple of hours.

Then she dialed again, glad that she'd managed to memorize this new number so quickly. "Hello, Cam?" she said when a familiar voice answered. "It's me. We finished early. Want to meet me at the stable?"

ELEVEN

Stevie was a little late meeting Cassidy at the town newspaper office. Those phone calls for Max had taken longer than she'd expected, and Cassidy was already poring over an old-fashioned microfiche machine when Stevie rushed in, breathless and red-faced from her jog in from the parking lot across the street. "Hi, sorry I'm late."

Cassidy glanced up at her and blinked. "No harm done," she said calmly. "Grab a seat. You can take that stack there." She gestured at a pile of cartridges beside the second microfiche machine.

Stevie picked up the top cartridge in the pile and wrinkled her nose at it. "Haven't these people ever heard of computers?" she commented. "Geez! Talk about the Stone Ages."

Cassidy smiled without looking up from the screen in front of her. "It would be easier if they'd finished updating their records," she agreed. "But we'll just have to make do."

With a sigh, Stevie planted herself in front of the

free microfiche machine. She'd never used one before, but it wasn't hard to figure out how to insert the cartridge and bring up the dim, slightly fuzzy images on the screen. Soon she was scanning local news stories from forty years earlier. Parades. Robberies. Elections. A tornado in the next county.

There were a couple of stories that mentioned Fenton Hall, though only briefly. As Stevie was dutifully jotting down the relevant details, Cassidy glanced over at her. "Don't forget to check the Milestones page."

"Why?" Stevie asked in surprise. The Milestones page of the *Gazette* was where wedding and birth announcements appeared, as well as obituaries and other personal items.

"Sometimes people mention their alma maters in those announcements," Cassidy explained patiently. "There may be something interesting there."

Fat chance, Stevie thought sourly. But she flipped back to the Milestones page, which she'd skipped in the first few issues on the microfiche. Sure enough, one old geezer had placed a notice announcing his retirement from teaching music at Fenton Hall. *Jackpot,* Stevie thought with a touch of sarcasm. She turned to note the information on her pad, then yanked the microfiche out of the machine and reached for the next one on the pile.

The issues on the new cartridge were slightly more recent, dating from thirteen years before. Stevie wondered idly if her parents had placed a birth announcement for her younger brother, Michael. Flipping to the correct month, she quickly found the Milestones page.

Michael wasn't mentioned, which didn't surprise Stevie too much. By their fourth kid, she figured, maybe her parents were over the whole newspaper announcement thing. She was about to move on when a photo near the bottom of the page caught her eye. She paused and stared at it, wondering why the smiling, attractive teenage girl with the wide, open smile and the sprinkling of freckles across her upturned nose looked so strangely familiar. Stevie frowned at the girl curiously, wondering who she was and why Stevie felt as if she knew her. She was about to give up, assuming that the girl was just another old neighbor or some acquaintance of her parents', when something suddenly clicked.

Of course! she thought. *She looks like a slightly older, female version of A.J.!*

"That's weird," Stevie muttered under her breath. She stared at the photo. The resemblance was eerie. The girl had A.J.'s snub nose and his sharp chin. It was impossible to tell her hair color from the black-and-white photo, of course, but it looked as if it could be the same distinctive deep auburn shade as A.J.'s. Stevie shook her head in amazement. "Totally weird," she breathed, barely noticing that Cassidy was shooting her a curious glance. "She looks enough like A.J. to be his . . ." Her voice trailed off as a possibility struck her.

It couldn't be. Stevie gulped, her mind reeling at what this might mean. She stared at the grainy photo on the microfiche, frozen with shock. It wasn't until Cassidy looked over again and asked if anything was wrong that Stevie remembered where she was.

"Oh!" Stevie forced a smile. "No. Uh, I just got caught up in, you know, the past." When Cassidy shrugged and returned her attention to her own work, Stevie grabbed her notebook and flipped to a clean page.

HELEN BARRETT, she wrote in large block letters. Beneath that she scribbled the date of the newspaper and a few other bits of information from the brief article beneath the photo, which announced that the smiling girl had just been accepted to a prestigious college in another state. Then she ripped out the page, folded it carefully, and tucked it into her pocket.

". . . and remember that hayride Dad arranged for my birthday?" Carole asked, whisking a few stray hairs off Starlight's face with a soft-bristled brush.

Cam chuckled. "I sure do," he said, reaching past Starlight's nose to tweak Carole on the chin. "You looked awfully cute with straw in your hair."

Carole giggled. She was starting to get used to hearing that sort of compliment from him. Well, sort of, anyway. "Oh yeah?" she retorted, dropping her brush and stooping to grab a handful of Starlight's bedding, which had drifted out into the aisle where the gelding was cross-tied. "Well, let's see how that look works on you!"

She leaped forward, aiming for Cam's close-cropped, curly black hair. Cam dodged just in time and grabbed her around the waist, swinging her around and then tickling her until she dropped the straw.

"No fair!" she panted, breathless from laughing. "This is supposed to be a no-tickling zone."

Just then she heard the sound of someone clearing her throat. Glancing up, she saw Rachel Hart standing in the aisle watching them, shifting uncertainly from one foot to the other.

"Oh!" Carole said, embarrassed to have one of the younger students catch her goofing off. She knew that a lot of the intermediate riders looked up to her, and she didn't want to set a bad example. "Um, hi, Rachel," she said, straightening her shirt collar, which had been knocked askew during the brief straw fight.

"Hi," Rachel replied, glancing quickly at Cam and blushing slightly.

Carole hid a smile. She couldn't really blame the

younger girl for staring—guys as good-looking as Cam didn't hang around Pine Hollow every day of the week. "What's up?" she asked the younger girl.

Rachel shrugged. "Oh, nothing," she said. "Um, my friends and I were just in the tack room talking about the Starlight Ride." She glanced wistfully at Starlight, who was giving Cam a suspicious look as he teased a few bits of straw out of the gelding's forelock. "May just told me how Starlight got his name," she added softly. "That's pretty cool. I heard you were the torchbearer that year, right?"

Carole nodded. She had been the torchbearer for several years before she'd graduated from the intermediate class, but she didn't bother to mention that. It would only sound like bragging, since the job of torchbearer was always given to the best overall intermediate or beginning rider for that year. "Uh-huh," she said instead. "It was a real honor to be picked. Who did Max choose this year?" Normally Carole would have known the answer, but that year, because of her grounding, she was a little out of touch with the day-to-day details of the stable.

Rachel was blushing again. "Me," she admitted. "I get to be the torchbearer this year. It's my first time."

"Congratulations!" Carole said, honestly happy for the younger girl. Rachel was a terrific rider and a terrific young horsewoman—she'd proved that by taking excellent care of Starlight during Carole's grounding. "You totally deserve it, Rachel. Really."

"Thanks." Rachel smiled bashfully, then shot a quick glance behind Carole.

For a second Carole thought that Rachel was looking at Cam. But then she realized she was actually peeking at Starlight.

Aha, Carole thought with a secret smile. *Now I'm starting to see what she's up to.*

"Hey, Rachel," she said, keeping her voice casual. "I just had a great idea. Why don't you ride Starlight in the Starlight Ride this year?"

Rachel gasped. "Really?" she asked, her voice so high and excited that it was almost a squeak. "You mean it, Carole?"

Carole nodded. "Absolutely," she declared. "Starlight would be totally honored to carry this year's torchbearer." Normally, as a Pine Hollow employee, Carole was expected to ride along with the younger students on the Starlight Ride. For the past couple of years, she and Ben and Denise had accompanied the riders to keep an eye on things and deal with any problems that arose on the trail while Max and Red drove into town with the hay and other refreshments. But this year Carole wasn't technically an employee anymore. She doubted that her father would allow her to go along, even for fun.

This way, Starlight will get to hold up the tradition

199

for both of us, she thought, smiling at the gleeful expression on Rachel's face as she gave the big bay gelding a hug. *And I know it would mean a lot to Rachel. She's almost as crazy about him as I am.*

"Thank you, Carole!" Rachel cried breathlessly. "Thank you, thank you! I have to go tell my friends about this!" She hugged Starlight once more, then raced off down the hall.

Just this once, Carole decided not to bother yelling after her to say that running wasn't allowed in the stable. Instead she turned to face Cam as Rachel scurried around the corner at the end of the aisle. To Carole's surprise, Cam didn't return her contented smile. In fact, his handsome face looked downright disapproving.

"What did you do that for?" he asked.

"What do you mean?" Carole raised both eyebrows in surprise. "She loves Starlight. It was totally obvious she was hinting around to be able to ride him on the big night. And she deserves to—she's really helped me out with him lately."

Cam didn't look convinced. "Whatever," he said. "I'm sure she's very deserving and all. It's just that, well, I was sort of hoping *we* could go on the Starlight Ride. You know, together." He stepped over and wrapped both arms around her, pulling her to him until their faces were only inches apart. "I thought it sounded very romantic," he murmured.

Carole felt her heart flutter, the way it always did

when she was so close to Cam. "Oh," she said breathlessly. "Um, it would be great if we could go together."

She let her eyes drift halfway shut, waiting for Cam to kiss her. But instead he merely shrugged and released her, turning back toward Starlight. "It just seems like you'd want to ride Starlight yourself," he muttered.

Carole was a little surprised that he would begrudge Rachel something that obviously meant so much to her. After all, he'd seen how excited she'd been at the idea of riding Starlight. But Carole didn't think about that for long. She was a little overwhelmed at the fact that he was already planning so far ahead—thinking about the two of them being together at Christmas. "It's no big deal," she said, hoping that he didn't think she wasn't as thrilled as he was at the idea of going on the Starlight Ride together. "It's just that I'm not sure Dad will let me go. But if he does, I'll just ride one of Max's horses. He won't mind."

Cam turned around again to face her. "Okay," he said with a slightly sheepish smile. "Sorry, I didn't mean to sound like a jerk or whatever. It's just that I want to grab any chance I can to be with you." He stepped toward her again, taking her hand and yanking her gently after him as he stepped backward into Starlight's open stall. "Like now, for instance."

Carole giggled and collapsed against him, turning her face up to meet his kiss. He slid one arm around her waist and turned, pressing her against the side wall of the stall as he covered her face with soft kisses. Carole's eyes were drifting shut when she heard the sound of footsteps and a snort from Starlight, who was still cross-tied outside. Her eyes flew open again. Cam's lips had moved on to her neck by then, and she glanced over his shoulder into the aisle, a little embarrassed at the thought of Max catching them making out. She was just in time to see Ben gliding past in the aisle outside. He didn't look their way, but Carole had the uncomfortable impression that he knew they were there. And that he knew exactly what they were doing.

Cam zeroed in on her lips again, but she ducked aside to avoid the kiss. "Um, we should stop," she whispered self-consciously. "Starlight . . ." She gestured vaguely in the direction of her horse.

Cam glanced out the stall door at Starlight, who was dozing contentedly in his cross-ties in the aisle. "He's fine. It won't hurt him to stand there for a few minutes."

"No, really." Carole couldn't quite bring herself to meet his gaze. "If Max comes by and sees him out there unattended, he'll freak."

Cam shrugged, looking slightly annoyed. But his tone was affable as he spoke. "All right, then let's get out there and attend to him. Lead the way."

They returned to their grooming, and a few minutes later Starlight was ready to return to his stall.

Once he was settled, Carole and Cam stowed the grooming equipment in the tack trunk in the aisle. Then they headed to the student locker room to pick up their jackets and street shoes.

The locker room was unoccupied, and Carole sat down in front of the row of cubbies to pull off her boots. Normally she kept her things in the stable office along with the rest of the staff. Now that she was on hiatus, she felt strange about doing that, so she was stowing a few things in her friends' cubbies. As she stood to toss her boots into Lisa's cubby, Cam sat down on the bench behind her.

"Okay," he said, grabbing her by the waist and spinning her around. "Now can we get back to what we were doing?"

This time Carole gave in without protest, collapsing limply onto Cam's lap in her stocking feet as he began nibbling enthusiastically on her earlobe. *Why not?* she thought a bit defiantly as she wrapped her arms around him. *Why should seeing Ben make me feel the least bit weird about being with Cam? Sure, maybe Ben and I kissed once. And maybe up until a few days ago I thought there was a chance we might be more than friends someday. But now I have Cam.*

"Oh, Carole," Cam murmured with feeling, nuzzling her cheek. "I'm crazy about you."

With a shiver, Carole turned her face slightly to capture his lips with her own. Cam kissed her back hungrily, burying his hands in her hair. As she sank into the kiss, the image of Ben danced into her mind once more, but this time she banished it quickly. *I don't need to worry about Ben Marlow anymore,* she thought dreamily. *Now I know what having a real boyfriend is like. And I like the feeling. Just like I like the feeling of kissing Cam. . . .*

TWELVE

"For the fifth time, I don't care which tie you wear tomorrow night." Callie rolled her eyes and glanced over at her brother from the passenger's seat of his car. "I seriously doubt Lisa will notice either way."

"You think?" Scott frowned at the windshield. "I guess the red one looks better. I'll have to ask Dad what he thinks. Maybe I can borrow one of his."

Callie stole another glance at her brother, a little surprised that he was obsessing so much over his wardrobe. He'd been talking about it since they'd left the house a few minutes earlier, headed for the next of Callie's appointments. It wasn't like him. *He didn't even get this worked up over what he was going to wear to the prom last year,* she thought. *Of course, it's not like there's too much thought involved when you're supposed to wear a tux. But still . . .*

She was beginning to wonder if there was more to this date than she'd thought. "So it should be fun," she commented casually. "The CARL thing, I mean."

"For sure," Scott replied enthusiastically, easing up on the gas as a panel truck shifted into the lane ahead of them. They were on local Highway 12, one of the main thoroughfares between Washington, D.C., and outlying towns like Willow Creek. The afternoon rush of commuters heading home from work was already starting, so Scott had to keep his eyes on the road. "It's going to be a blast. Especially now that I'm going with Lisa. I just hope she has a good time."

"I'm sure she will," Callie replied automatically.

That's four times he's mentioned her name in the past ten minutes, she thought. *Or is it five times? I've lost track.*

"She'd better." Scott chuckled. "Otherwise I'm going to have a tough time convincing her to go out with me again."

Now Callie was sure this was no ordinary date. Her brother wasn't the type to plan ahead—not when it came to girls, at least. "Wow," she said. At Scott's surprised glance, she quickly added, "I just hope Stevie's not too disappointed."

"Huh?"

Callie winced, realizing too late what she'd said. "Oh, nothing," she said quickly.

But Scott was looking over at her again, his blue eyes concerned. "What was that about Stevie?" he asked. "She's not upset because of the whole Alex thing. Is she? I'd hate to think that I—"

"No, no—and keep your eyes on the road!" Callie said hastily, wishing she'd just kept her mouth shut. Now she was going to have to tell him the truth, or he'd worry endlessly that Stevie was upset with him. He might even confront her about it, and then Callie would really feel like an idiot. "It's not about that," she told her brother. "It's just that, well—" She hesitated, turning to stare at him. "You have to swear you won't let on that you know."

"Know what?" Scott asked.

Callie sighed. "Okay. Um, Stevie noticed that you've been hanging around Pine Hollow a lot lately, even though you don't usually ride. And I guess you two must run into each other a lot at school, and I guess she thought that was your doing, too. So she sort of thought—well, she somehow got the idea that you had a crush on her."

Scott blinked, looking confused for a moment. Then he laughed. "Really?" he cried delightedly. "Stevie thought that I— Oh, that's too much!" He burst out laughing in earnest.

Callie shot him an uncertain glance. She wasn't entirely sure she trusted him to keep quiet. When it came to really important secrets, or ones that could hurt someone if they came out, Scott was a vault. But he was much more easily tempted by juicy little secrets like this one, ones that he judged more humorous than hurtful. And she was afraid that this one would fall squarely into the former category. Scott and Stevie enjoyed teasing each other, and this would give him plenty of ammunition.

She opened her mouth to remind him that he had to keep quiet, but before she could say a word, Scott hit his turn signal. "We're here," he said.

Glancing ahead, Callie saw the massive red barn of Fair Acres Farm. She had driven past this particular property dozens of times on the way to the airport or her father's office in the city. But until she'd begun her search for a new endurance horse, she hadn't realized that Fair Acres even had any horses. She'd thought they dealt exclusively in beef cattle.

I hope this isn't a waste of time, she thought, glancing out the side window at a herd of grazing Herefords as Scott turned up the drive. *Still, Denise saw this horse, and she swore it has endurance potential. And she usually knows what she's talking about.*

That made her feel a little more optimistic. Denise McCaskill was one of the most knowledgeable horsewomen Callie had ever met, and she respected her opinion. If she thought this horse had potential, it was definitely worth a look.

"Looks like we can park over there." Callie pointed to a small turnaround where a couple of pickup trucks and a white sedan were parked.

As Scott cut the ignition, Callie was already releasing her seat belt and opening her door. As she climbed out of the car, she caught sight of someone hurrying toward them from the barn. She closed the door behind her and turned, already smiling automatically in greeting.

The smile froze on her face as she recognized the figure heading their way. "George!" she gasped in shock. "What are you doing here?"

George was grinning broadly as he reached the Foresters, his moon-shaped face the picture of self-satisfied glee. "Surprise!" he cried. "I remembered you were coming here today to look at a horse, and I figured I'd stop by in case you needed a second opinion."

Callie was so stunned that all she could do was open her mouth and close it again. She glanced helplessly at Scott, who looked startled and slightly worried. *I can't believe George is here,* Callie thought. *I can't believe how totally inappropriate and weird this is.*

"Hello!" a new voice called. "You must be the folks come to look at the horse."

Callie turned and saw a tall, rail-thin man striding toward them, a ten-gallon hat on his head and a welcoming smile on his weather-beaten face. "Hello," she said, her mind still too numb from the shock of George's unexpected appearance to manage anything more.

"This is Callie," George said, putting a hand on her arm and smiling at the man, then turning his smile in her direction. "Callie, this is Mr. Rayburn. He and his wife own this place. We were just chatting while we were waiting for you, and I told him all about your endurance experience and everything."

Scott stepped forward and extended his hand to Mr. Rayburn, in the process managing to move between Callie and George and knock George's hand loose of Callie's arm. Callie glanced at her brother gratefully as he greeted the farm owner jovially and suggested they head right in to see the horse.

What in the world does George think he's doing? Callie thought furiously as the entire group trooped into the big red barn. *He's acting like I invited him along or something. No, worse than that. He's acting like he* belongs *here. Like it's totally natural for him to show up like this.*

She gritted her teeth as George started telling Mr. Rayburn about the Foresters' move from the West Coast. What made him think he had the right to barge in on her life all the time? She'd made it perfectly clear that she needed some space. Why couldn't he seem to understand that?

Soon they stopped in front of a large stall where a rangy little leopard-spot Appaloosa gelding was munching on a rack full of hay. "This here's Scooby," Mr. Rayburn said proudly. "Tough as nails and sweet as sugar, as my wife likes to say."

Callie smiled politely, but she hardly even saw the horse standing in front of her. She was too busy trying not to start screaming at George right there in front of the farm owner.

Keep it under control, girl, she told herself firmly,

stepping forward automatically to pat Scooby on the neck. *Just get through this.*

She noticed Scott shooting her worried glances as Mr. Rayburn chatted about the horse, seeming unaware of the tension. George, too, seemed completely oblivious as he stood by with his hands clasped behind his back, smiling complacently.

Somehow Callie managed to maintain control as she stepped into the stall to take a closer look, though she didn't take in a word that the farm owner was telling her about Scooby. Finally Mr. Rayburn tacked up the horse and led him outside for Callie to try.

Callie was relieved for the chance to swing into the saddle and escape from George, at least momentarily. As she leaned over to adjust her stirrups, she stole a quick look at him. He had walked outside with the others and was gazing at her innocently, as if there were nothing strange about this whole situation.

He's going to figure out otherwise soon enough, she thought grimly as she signaled for a walk. The horse obeyed, though Callie doubted she would have noticed if he'd decided to trot or gallop or levitate instead. *As soon as we're finished here, I'm going to give him a piece of my mind. This is it. It ends here, once and for all.*

She had tightened her grip on the reins without realizing it. Scooby shook his head and flicked his dark-tipped ears back at her. "Sorry," Callie murmured, loosening the reins and asking for a trot.

Seeming relieved, the horse obliged, his surprisingly long stride carrying them quickly across the paddock. When Callie turned him at the far end, she glanced at her little audience. George was talking to Mr. Rayburn again, and she shuddered to think what he might be saying.

Probably inviting him to our wedding, she thought with a twisted smile.

She forced herself to ride around the paddock for a few more minutes, not wanting to insult Mr. Rayburn. Scooby was probably a very good horse, but Callie was sure she was too distracted to pay much attention even if she were riding Pegasus himself.

Finally she pulled up at the paddock gate. "Thank you," she told Mr. Rayburn politely as she swung out of the saddle. Once on the ground, she patted Scooby on his spotted side. "He seems great. I'll have to think about it and let you know."

"Fair enough," Mr. Rayburn replied, already reaching to run up the stirrups. "I'm always here if you have questions or want to try him again."

Relieved that Scooby's owner wasn't going to try giving her the hard sell, Callie quickly said good-bye and headed back to the car, doing her best to keep her hands from shaking with fury. Behind her, she heard her brother launching into a more elaborate thank you and farewell, covering up her rudeness.

She was sure she would be grateful to him later, but at the moment the only emotion she felt was pure, hot, seething rage.

When she reached Scott's car, she took a deep breath and spun around. As expected, George had trailed along behind her, huffing and puffing as he tried to keep up. He stopped short and blinked at her, obviously noticing her furious expression.

"What's wrong, Callie?" he asked uncertainly. "Didn't the horse seem—"

"Shut up and listen to me," Callie hissed, not letting him finish. "I'm sick and tired of this. When are you going to get it through your thick head that I mean it when I say I want you to stay away from me?"

George's eyes were wide with surprise. "But Callie," he protested. "I was only trying to help. I thought—"

"I don't need your help," she cut him off sharply. "And I definitely don't need to keep having this same conversation with you over and over again. It's like you don't pay any attention at all to what I want or need—how inconsiderate is that? Not to mention insulting."

"Okay, I understand, and I'm sorry," George said quickly, holding his hands up in a gesture of appeasement. "Now, why don't we just forget about this and I'll try to do better. Okay?"

"No. That's not working," Callie snapped.

She was doing her best to keep her voice low, though it wasn't easy. A quick glance showed her that Scott had managed to steer Mr. Rayburn and Scooby back toward the barn, pretty well out of earshot.

Crossing her arms over her chest, she turned her attention back to George, glaring at him evenly. "So here's the new rule. There's only one, so you should be able to remember it. This friendship is hereby officially over. Finished. Just stay away from me, okay?"

George stood quietly for a moment, his expression blank. Finally he shrugged and sighed, shifting his gaze to a spot somewhere over Callie's left shoulder. "I'm sorry you feel that way," he said, his voice calm and emotionless.

Callie blinked in surprise. She had been steeling herself for tears, hysteria, begging. . . . She never would have expected that George would have no reaction at all.

Before she could decide what to think about that, George turned away. Moving amazingly fast, he walked over to the white car parked nearby, climbed in, and pulled the door shut behind him. Seconds later the car was disappearing around the corner at the end of the drive.

Callie collapsed against Scott's car, relief flooding through her. It was over. George could have no question now how she felt. Thinking back over their bizarre friendship, she couldn't help feeling guilty and a little unsettled. It really had been strange how he hadn't even tried to change her mind.

Forget about it, she told herself firmly, standing up straight and looking around for her brother so that they could get going. *I'm just glad this whole stupid, pathetic thing is finished at last.*

Lisa picked up her mother's favorite blue china vase and stared at it for a moment before replacing it in its spot on the living-room mantel. It looked so nice there against the grain of the wood. How would it look in some strange house miles and miles away?

She glanced around the room, taking in every familiar detail as if seeing it for the first time. This was the house she'd grown up in. The only house she could remember. It was her home. Willow Creek was her home.

I can't believe Mom is even thinking about moving, she thought helplessly, rubbing her eyes with one hand. *It's totally unreal. This has got to be one of her passing whims, like the time she started collecting stamps, or last spring when she decided to take up yoga.*

She certainly hoped that was the case. Her mother wasn't known for her follow-through, and Lisa figured there was at least a fighting chance that she'd forget all about the idea of moving to New Jersey by the time she got home from work that night. That was why Lisa hadn't bothered to call her friends yet to tell them what her mother had said. What good would it do to get them all worked up for nothing?

"I just wish she hadn't kept talking about it at dinner," Lisa muttered aloud, walking over to the coffee table and picking up a crystal bowl full of potpourri. She stared at it blindly, picturing the cramped suburb in New Jersey where her aunt's family lived.

"We can find a nice place near your aunt Marianne's," her mother had chirped cheerfully as she'd dumped ranch dressing on her salad. "Marianne and I have been talking about this for a long time now—since last summer, actually. I got sidetracked from the idea for a while, but now . . ." She'd shrugged, clearly not wanting to get any further into the topic of her recently ended romance.

Lisa had started to protest, listing all sorts of reasons why such a move was a bad idea, starting with the fact that she was halfway through her senior year. But her mother hadn't seemed interested in a family discussion.

"It might be good for you to have a change of scenery, Lisa," she'd said with a slightly disapproving frown. "It could give you a fresh perspective, help you put your life into balance and realize why we're all so upset about this college situation of yours."

Lisa shuddered and set down the bowl of potpourri, wondering how her mother could be so totally wrapped up in her own problems that she couldn't even see how horrible it would be for Lisa to have to pack up and leave behind her friends, her school, Pine Hollow, and everything else she'd always known.

"It's insane," she muttered, wandering out into the hall. "Totally insane. Of course, Mom hasn't exactly been Ms. Rational lately."

It wasn't a comforting thought. *I'm going to be turning eighteen in just a few months,* Lisa thought plaintively. *I'm almost a legal adult. Shouldn't I have some say in my own life by now?*

"Okay." Stevie took a deep breath and stared at Phil. "Let's do it."

Phil nodded briefly. "Come on."

He led the way into the main building of Cross County Stables. Stevie felt her stomach flip-flop nervously as they headed for the stall where Crystal, A.J.'s horse, was housed. She'd been having anxious jitters ever since finding that picture in the old newspaper earlier that day. She had called Phil as soon as she'd arrived home from the *Gazette*'s office, and the two of them had discussed it for more than half an hour before deciding they should tell A.J. in person.

By the time they'd reached A.J.'s house, he'd already left for the stable. Not wanting to wait around until he returned, they'd headed over to Cross County to track him down.

They found him in Crystal's stall, picking out her

feet. "Hey, guys," he greeted them in surprise, dropping the mare's left forefoot and straightening up to stretch. "What are you two doing here?"

"Looking for you," Phil replied soberly. "Listen, A.J. We have something to tell you. Something we think you should know."

Stevie took a deep breath, plunging right in before A.J. could ask any more questions. "Listen, A.J. I found something interesting while I was doing some research today . . ." She went on to describe the photo and explain what she'd thought when she saw it. "There's no guarantee it's really your birth mother or anything," she finished. "But I think it's worth checking out. This Helen Barrett really looks an awful lot like you. And who knows?"

She paused for breath, giving A.J. a careful look to see how he was taking it all. He hadn't said a word since she'd started, though he had moved to the front of the stall. His freckles stood out starkly against his face, which had gone pale.

"A.J.?" Phil said worriedly. "Are you okay?"

"I don't know," A.J. said slowly, clutching his hoof pick tightly in one hand. His eyes were troubled and confused. "This is all so—I guess I just need to think about it for a while."

Stevie bit the inside of her cheek to keep herself from blurting out all kinds of questions: *Are you going to try to track her down? Do you think it really could be your mother?* But she knew that would be sticking her nose in where it didn't belong. It was up to A.J. to take the next step.

Phil cleared his throat. "Let us know if you need any help," he told A.J. "You know."

Stevie nodded. She really hoped that A.J. would pursue this clue. *Maybe finding his birth mother will help him make peace with his past,* she thought hopefully. *And maybe then he can figure out a way to deal with the present.* She thought briefly of Julianna before returning her full attention to A.J.

"So are you going to—" Stevie began, then stopped herself. No, she wasn't going to pry. She quickly came up with a save. "Uh, are you going to the CARL thing tomorrow night?"

A.J. looked surprised at the sudden change of topic, but he shrugged. "I don't know. I guess so."

"Good." Stevie gave Phil a look. If they could get A.J. out having fun with his friends, maybe that would help him deal with this new information. Because there didn't seem to be much more they could do for him now one way or the other. Not until he made up his mind about whether or not he wanted to face his true past.

In the meantime, all she could do was head home for dinner. It had been a long day, and she was starving.

THIRTEEN

On her way into homeroom the next morning, Stevie reached down and grabbed a copy of the week's *Sentinel* out of the basket just inside the classroom door. She made her way to her usual seat, nodding hello to a few of her classmates as she passed. She noticed vaguely that Kenny Lamb had an even stranger look on his face than usual as he returned her greeting, and Wesley Ward just started laughing when she gave him a quick wave.

Stevie shrugged. For some reason, people always seemed to get a little wacky on Fridays.

She dropped her books on her desk and sat down. Unfolding the newspaper, she glanced at the headlines on the front page. Basketball tryouts bring record turnout. New walk-in freezer in the cafeteria. Controversy over some new zoning law in town.

Stevie rolled her eyes. *Give me a break,* she thought. *I could come up with a more interesting story than these with my pen tied behind my back.*

"Hi, Stevie," Betsy Cavanaugh said, walking over

to her desk with a funny little smirk on her face. "Got today's *Sentinel* there, huh?"

Stevie raised an eyebrow as she glanced up. "No," she replied sarcastically. "It's last Thursday's London *Times.*" She shook her head as the other girl burst out laughing and hurried away. Betsy had always been kind of a flake, even back in the days when she'd ridden at Pine Hollow.

Returning her attention to her newspaper, Stevie flipped to the second page and scanned the letters to the editor and the update on the previous week's PTA meeting. As she glanced at the sports scores on the opposite page, she kept getting distracted by loud snorts of laughter. Glancing up in irritation, she caught several people staring at her, but they all looked away quickly when she caught them at it, hiding their faces behind their own copies of the *Sentinel* and giggling wildly.

Stevie frowned. What was going on?

Suddenly she felt a sharp pang of suspicion. *Wait a minute,* she thought, flipping quickly through the rest of the paper. *I almost forgot. Today is Veronica's big gossip debut.*

She found Veronica's column on the second-to-last page. " 'In the Hall,' " the title line read, "by Veronica diAngelo."

Skimming the first couple of paragraphs, Stevie started to relax. It was pretty much what she would have expected—boring gossip about who had appeared at the latest hot parties, rumors of breakups and makeups among members of Veronica's cliquey crowd, and a thinly veiled reference to Mr. Carpenter's new hairpiece.

Then she reached the final paragraph. As she read through it, her jaw tightened and her head started to throb. Wondering if she could possibly be hallucinating—maybe Veronica's boring gossip about her cronies had brought on a stroke or something—Stevie read the last part of the column again.

This reporter heard another juicy tidbit in the hall this week, it read, Veronica's smug, superior attitude practically oozing out of every word. *Much as it disgusts one to think that a supposedly well-respected member of the Fenton Hall student government could be a repulsive trash picker, this reporter saw a certain female junior pulling a certain item of food out of the Dumpster behind the gym. She then proceeded to shove the whole thing in her mouth and gobble it down like a prisoner gulping her last meal. I won't give any names to protect the taste-challenged, but suffice it to say that the snack in question was a SuperCrunch granola bar.*

Stevie clenched her fist so hard that the page ripped slightly at the edge. Everyone at Fenton Hall knew that SuperCrunch granola bars were Stevie's favorite food—she'd passed them out with her picture wrapped around them to advertise her campaign for student government the previous spring. It wouldn't be hard for most people to figure out the identity of the unnamed student government member in Veronica's ridiculous made-up story—including, apparently, the majority of people in Stevie's homeroom.

But there was more. Stevie swallowed her anger and forced herself to read on.

On a lighter note, this reporter is happy to note that love is in the air for a certain popular junior, Miss N, who has been seen locking lips with a certain brown-haired, hazel-eyed basketball- and soccer-playing junior. Kudos to Miss N's new flame for finally getting some taste! In other romantic revelations, a reputable source reports that everyone's favorite student body president has an eye for a certain student body—the buzz is, it's his old campaign manager! I guess it's true what they say—politics makes for strange bedfellows. . . .

Stevie's face was burning by the time she finished reading. Crumpling the paper into a ball, she smashed it under her Spanish textbook. Veronica had gone too far this time. And Stevie was going to make her pay.

She fumed through the rest of homeroom, counting the seconds until she could escape and wreak horrible revenge. Strangulation came immediately to mind. Then beheading. As soon as the bell rang, she leaped from her seat and raced out into the hall, heading for Veronica's homeroom a few doors down. She was waiting when Veronica emerged a moment later, chatting with several friends.

"Yo, diAngelo," Stevie snapped. "I want to talk to you."

Veronica smirked. "Sorry, no autographs," she said breezily. "If you want to congratulate me on my column, just get in line." A few passing students heard the comment and laughed, pausing and looking curiously at Stevie.

Stevie ignored them and took a step closer to her foe. "Not funny, Veronica," she said, her voice rising with anger. "How dare you print those stupid lies about me and my friends in your so-called column?" A crowd was gathering as students heading to their first classes stopped to see what all the shouting was about. Within seconds people were jostling for position, craning their necks to see. Stevie noticed that her brother and Nicole were among those standing near Veronica.

Meanwhile Veronica shrugged, extending one hand and examining her perfectly shaped fingernails as she replied, "It's not lies, Stevie. It's gossip. Need a dictionary to understand what that means?"

"Here's a dictionary word for you," Stevie barked. "*Libel*. Look it up. Then maybe you'll be ready to print a retraction to that garbage you wrote."

"Garbage?" Nicole spoke up with a snicker. "Did you say something about garbage, Stevie? But it's not even lunchtime yet!"

Stevie gritted her teeth at the laughter from the crowd. She was vaguely aware that Alex was one of the few people not cracking up at Nicole's comment. He looked uncomfortable.

"I mean it, Veronica." Stevie pointedly ignored everyone else, focusing her glare fully on Veronica. "I want a retraction. A big one."

"No way." Veronica crossed her arms over her chest and turned up her nose. "You can't control what I write, Stevie. Freedom of the press and all that."

Stevie clutched her forehead, feeling like she was going to scream. "What a joke!" she yelled. "The only freedom you need is the freedom to be a total—" Just in time, she spotted Mr. Dewey, the Latin teacher, hurrying toward them. "A total jerk," she finished lamely.

"What's going on here?" Mr. Dewey demanded, wading through the crowd until he reached Veronica and Stevie. Glancing from one girl to the other, he frowned. "What's the meaning of this?"

Veronica shrugged. "I don't know," she replied coolly. "I was just walking out of my homeroom when she ran up and starting yelling at me."

"It's nothing," Stevie told the teacher, forcing herself to sound calm. "Just a little disagreement. Sorry if we got loud."

Mr. Dewey looked skeptical, but he shrugged and glanced around. "Okay, break it up," he commanded, shooing the students away. "Get to class, all of you."

Veronica started to wander off, but as soon as Mr. Dewey disappeared back into his classroom, Stevie stomped after her and grabbed her by the arm. "This isn't over," she hissed. "You'd better go to Theresa right away and tell her you want to print a retraction in next week's issue, or there's going to be major trouble."

Veronica shook off her hand. "Give it up, Stevie," she snapped. "There's not going to be any retraction. In fact, I can't wait to get started on next week's column, and I'll write about whoever I want to in that one, too. So deal with it."

Stevie clenched her fists. "Fine," she called as Veronica continued down the hall. "If that's the way you want it, I'll play. This is war!"

Without waiting for a response, she spun around and stomped off toward her first class. If Veronica thought she was going to let this go without a fight, she was sadly mistaken.

That evening Carole stood in front of the open door of her bedroom closet staring at the clothes hanging inside. She had just come upstairs to get ready for the CARL party, only to realize that she had no idea what to wear. Normally she wouldn't have thought much about it one way or the other—she would have thrown on whatever was clean and that would be that. But tonight was different. She wanted to look her best for Cam.

"Don't I have any, like, dresses in here?" she muttered, reaching out and flipping past a couple of rat-catcher shirts, her good navy riding jacket, and several carefully hung pairs of breeches. "I know I used to have some dresses. Or skirts. Or something."

By digging past her riding clothes to the far reaches of the closet, she finally managed to strike gold. *Aha!* she thought in triumph, dragging out several slightly rumpled dresses. *I knew they were in here somewhere.*

She walked over to the bed and laid them out. Stepping back, she looked them over, trying to decide which one to wear. They all seemed pretty much the same to her. Which one would Cam like the best?

Carole chewed on her lower lip, staring from one dress to the other. "Maybe I should just close my eyes and point to one," she murmured. Checking her watch, she gulped nervously. She had to hurry if she wanted to have any time left to fix her hair and put on some makeup.

It was time to call in some reinforcements. Carole hurried out into the hall and leaned over the railing. "Dad?" she called. "Can I call Lisa?"

Her father wandered into sight at the foot of the stairs, his reading glasses on his nose and the newspaper in his hand. "Well, I don't know . . . ," he began.

"Please?" Carole cried. "I know I'm not supposed to make unnecessary phone calls, but this is an emergency." He still looked doubtful, so she added, "A *fashion* emergency."

Colonel Hanson's face cleared. "Ah," he said wisely. "In that case, go ahead. But keep it short, okay?"

"Don't worry," Carole said. "It'll definitely be short. Cam's supposed to pick me up in half an hour."

"Oh yes, Cam." Her father smiled, looking pleased. "Well, hurry up, then. I'll try to stall him if he arrives early."

Carole raced into her father's bedroom and grabbed the cordless phone from his bedside table. Heading back into her own room as she dialed, she was standing in front of her bed by the time Lisa picked up. "Crisis," Carole said briskly. "What do I wear?"

Like the true friend that she was, Lisa didn't need any further explanation. "What are the options?"

Carole studied the four dresses draped over her bed. "There's this sort of pinkish dress, but I think last time I wore it the skirt was kind of tight," she said. "Um, and this blue one—"

"Do you still have the green dress you wore to the Lakes' anniversary party last spring?" Lisa interrupted.

Carole nodded, then realized that Lisa couldn't see her through the phone. "Yes," she said, grabbing the dress in question and holding it up in front of her dresser mirror. "Do you think I should wear that one?"

"Definitely," Lisa said firmly. "It's got that full skirt that will be great for dancing, and the color really looks good against your skin."

"Thanks." Carole smiled at her reflection in the mirror, deciding that Lisa was right. The dress was perfect. She dropped it back on the bed and began shedding her clothes, the phone tucked into the crook of her shoulder. "So what are you going to wear?"

Lisa didn't answer for a moment. "What?" she said at last.

Carole paused as she switched the phone to the other ear. "I said, what are you wearing tonight?" she repeated, unzipping the green dress and stepping into it.

"Oh." Lisa sounded a little distracted. "Um, I guess my pink dress from the vintage shop."

"Cool. Scott will love it." The phone slipped out of Carole's grip, landing on the floor with a thunk, as she shimmied into the dress. Wriggling and yanking the dress the rest of the way up, she stooped and retrieved the phone. "Lisa? Are you still there? Sorry about that."

"Uh-huh. It's okay."

Carole frowned. Her friend definitely sounded weird. Suddenly Carole realized what the reason must be. "Lisa?" she said hesitantly. "You're not, like, really *nervous* about this date with Scott tonight, are you?"

"No, no, it's not that," Lisa said quickly. "It's just—um, can you keep a secret?"

"You know I can," Carole replied, opening the top drawer of her dresser and pawing through the jumble of socks and underwear inside, searching for a run-free pair of pantyhose. It would be chilly out that evening, and Carole didn't want to go bare-legged if she could help it. The party was being held in a large tent set up on the CARL grounds. A fancy, heated tent, but a tent nonetheless. "What is it?" she asked Lisa, a little distracted as she finally located a promising-looking pair.

Lisa took a deep breath that was audible even through the phone. "It's something Mom told me yesterday afternoon," she said. "She says she wants us to move to New Jersey to be near my aunt's family. And she wants us to do it right after New Year's."

Carole sank down onto the edge of the bed, her eyes wide with shock and disbelief. "No!" she exclaimed. "Move? You're kidding, right?"

"I wish," Lisa replied grimly. "I was sort of holding off on telling anyone because I figured it was just one of Mom's two-second obsessions. But she's still talking about it. She spent an hour on the phone with Aunt Marianne this afternoon."

"Yikes," Carole said succinctly. "But are you sure

she's really serious? I mean, she can't just expect you to—" She cut herself off as the sound of the doorbell echoed through the house. "Uh-oh. Could that be Cam already?"

"Go ahead," Lisa said with a sigh. "We can talk about this later. We have plenty of time." She let out a brief, slightly bitter laugh. "After all, I'm not moving for at least two and a half weeks, right?"

Carole opened her mouth to protest further— there had to be some mistake, Lisa's mother couldn't actually be thinking of moving now—when her father's voice floated up the stairs. "Carole! Cam's here."

"Oops, I guess I should go," Carole said apologetically. "Um, we'll talk later." She said good-bye, hit the Off button to hang up, and tossed the phone onto her pillow. Then she realized she was still holding the pair of pantyhose. Slipping them on quickly, she was relieved to find that they didn't have any runs or snags. She hurried to the bedroom door and stuck her head out. "I'll be right there," she called in what she hoped was a cheerful, casual tone. Then she raced over to her dresser and grabbed a tube of mascara, meanwhile casting a critical look at her hair. She'd taken it out of its usual braid, and it hung in loose ringlets down her back. The natural look would have to do—she didn't have time to fuss with it now.

After the world's fastest makeup application and some quick work with a hairbrush, Carole emerged from her room, still thinking more about what Lisa had just told her than about the coming evening's party.

I know Mrs. Atwood has been kind of nuts lately, but this is out of control, she thought as she started down the stairs, holding on to the railing to keep from slipping in her best dressy shoes. *How can she do this to Lisa? It's practically child abuse.*

At that moment she glanced up and saw Cam standing near the front door with her father, both of them watching her descent. She gulped, almost missing the next step as she got a good look at Cam. He looked positively incredible in his elegant dark suit and crimson tie.

"Wow, Carole," Cam said, stepping forward with a slightly shy smile. "You look . . . *amazing.*"

"That goes double for me, honey," her father said, stepping forward to help her down the last couple of steps. "You look beautiful. Now, you kids have a good time, okay?" He winked at Cam. "Don't keep her out all night."

"I won't, sir." Cam offered a mock salute, which made Colonel Hanson chuckle. Then he turned back to Carole and took her by the hand. "I feel like the luckiest guy on the planet," he murmured, leaning down to kiss her on the cheek. "You really are beautiful, you know."

"Thanks," Carole replied softly. "You—You look really nice, too." She didn't know how to tell him what she really wanted to say: that she, too, felt incredibly lucky. Lucky to have a great guy like him. Being with him made everything seem a little brighter, and made all the other problems in her life—her grounding, the loss of her job at Pine Hollow, and even Lisa's latest, horrible news—seem like they just might turn out okay after all.

She put on her coat and Cam led her out to his Jeep, which was parked at the curb just beyond the Hansons' driveway. "Ladies first," he said gallantly, opening the passenger's door for her.

Carole climbed in and started to pull down her seat belt. Meanwhile, Cam had hurried around to the driver's side.

"Wait," he said as he climbed in. "Don't put that on just yet. It will make it too hard for us to do this." With that, he looped one hand behind her neck and pulled her toward him for a long, deep kiss.

Yes, I think all that other stuff might just turn out okay in the end, Carole thought dreamily as she kissed him back, hardly noticing the gearshift digging into her thigh as she leaned across it. *When I feel like this, how could I possibly believe that anything really bad could ever happen?*

FOURTEEN

"Here we are," Scott said, cutting the ignition. "Sit tight, I'll get the door."

He hopped out of the driver's seat and hurried around to the passenger's side of his car. Lisa waited for him to open her door, feeling slightly disconcerted. Pulling open the door with a flourish, Scott offered his hand. Lisa took it as she climbed out of the car, trying not to notice how handsome he looked in his coat and tie.

This is bizarre, she thought as Scott leaned past her to close the door. *I see Scott all the time. Practically every day. So why does it feel as if we just met for the first time tonight?*

They were right on time, but it had still been difficult to find a parking spot on the streets surrounding the CARL facility. Scott had finally found an open spot three blocks away, so they had to walk to get to the party. Lisa pulled her dressy velvet coat closer around herself as they walked. It was already dark, and a cold breeze was raising gooseflesh on every bit of exposed skin.

Scott glanced at her. "Are you cold?" he asked with concern, reaching over and placing his hand protectively on the small of her back. "Do you want my jacket?"

"No, I'm okay." Lisa glanced up at him with a smile. "Thanks." She'd always noticed and appreciated Scott's smooth, charming way of dealing with people. But somehow, it felt different now that all of that attention was focused on her. It was kind of nice, but kind of weird at the same time. Not unpleasant—just different.

The sound of music drifted toward them on the next puff of wind. Scott glanced ahead. "Sounds like the party's started," he commented. He looked at her with a rakish grin. "I hope you're in the mood for dancing."

Lisa couldn't help being very aware that he hadn't removed his hand from her back. "Absolutely," she said, returning his smile. "I love dancing."

Not unpleasant at all, she thought with a shiver that had nothing to do with the wind.

"Isn't this amazing?" Stevie cried, grabbing Phil's hand and dragging him along after her as she wandered through the huge, brightly lit party tent, trying to take in everything at once. "Look how many people came!"

Phil nodded. "It's great," he agreed. "CARL should raise a lot of money." The fund-raiser had started only twenty minutes earlier, but the place was already packed with people. The warm breath and body heat of more than two hundred partyers had chased away whatever chill had been left by the busily pumping space heaters in the corners of the tent.

"I just hope they play some decent tunes," A.J. put in, following the others with his hands shoved deep in the pockets of his freshly pressed khakis. "I thought you guys promised me there'd be some boogeying going down tonight."

Stevie rolled her eyes and snorted, but secretly she was glad that A.J. seemed to be in a good mood. She was in a pretty good mood herself. It was a relief to have a night off from her two big jobs. If anyone was more of a slave driver than Cassidy, with her obsessive attention to every last boring detail, it was Max. He'd kept her hopping for several hours that afternoon preparing for the Starlight Ride.

"Hey, isn't that Roger over there?" Phil said, dropping Stevie's hand and poking A.J. in the shoulder. "Let's go say hi."

At that moment Stevie was distracted by the sound of a bark from the back of the tent. "I'll catch up with you," she told the guys. They nodded and hurried off to talk to their friend, while Stevie made a beeline for the source of the bark.

When she reached the back of the tent, she found that several of CARL's furry residents were holding court in a small, cordoned-off section near one of the heaters. "Hello," said a pleasant-looking middle-aged woman who was wearing a large button reading Ask Me About Volunteering. "I'm Natalie."

Stevie introduced herself politely, then squinted curiously at one of the dogs. He was a large mixed breed, mostly yellow with some brown patches. His muzzle was white with age and his movements were a little stiff, but his rapidly wagging tail looked very familiar.

"Don't tell me," Stevie said. "Champ?"

The old dog let out a sharp bark at the sound of his name and his tail whipped back and forth faster than ever. Panting eagerly, he submitted happily to Stevie's hug and chest scratches.

Natalie smiled. "That's right," she said. "I guess this means you've visited CARL before."

"Last Saturday was the first time in years," Stevie admitted. "But Champ was here when I was here . . . gee, must've been four or five years ago."

The woman nodded and smiled at Champ fondly. "He's been our mascot for a long time." She gestured at the other animals. One was a large gray tabby cat, snoozing away in a wire animal crate in front of the blower of the large heater. "That's Bubba," Natalie said, indicating the cat. "And this is Freckles." She patted the second dog.

"He looks like a purebred Dalmatian," Stevie said in surprise, offering her hand for Freckles to sniff and then giving him a pat.

"He is," Natalie confirmed. "We get a lot of purebreds, especially of the larger, more popular breeds. A lot of people think you'll only find mutts in shelters, but that's just not true."

"Wow." Stevie stroked Freckles's smooth black-and-white fur, wishing she could take him home. But she knew if she did, her parents would have a stroke.

As if reading her mind, Natalie asked, "Does your family have any pets?"

"I have a horse named Belle," Stevie replied. "And my family has a dog. He's a golden retriever. We got him from someone my dad works with—they have two goldens, and one plus one turned out to equal eleven. They had nine puppies."

"Ah." Instead of laughing, Natalie looked rather sad. "That's where we get a lot of our animals, too. People don't realize that letting their pet have a litter—accidental or not, purebred or not—adds immensely to the population of unwanted animals, like Freckles here. That's one of the causes we're raising money for tonight. We want to expand our low-cost spay/neuter program to make it easier for people to be responsible. A lot of other shelters are offering similar programs."

"Don't worry," Stevie said hastily. The woman's lecture was interesting, but it made Stevie feel bad for all those unwanted puppies and kittens out there. "Bear is already neutered."

"Good." The woman smiled. Just then an older couple wandered up wanting to pet the animals, so Stevie looked around for Phil and A.J.

Phil was nowhere in sight, but A.J. was talking with friends nearby. *He looks like he's having fun,* she thought, watching him as he laughed and made a funny face in response to something one of his friends had just said. *I wonder if he decided what to do about Helen Barrett yet?*

She wished she could march right over and ask him. But the last thing she wanted to do was keep bugging him about it. That wouldn't accomplish anything.

It's his life. And it's got to be his decision whether to pursue this or not, she thought. Just then she noticed a flash of pink from the dance floor. Glancing over, she saw Lisa and Scott doing a professional-looking fox-trot right along with several much older couples. *Sort of like it was Lisa and Alex's decision to start dating other people,* Stevie added to herself as she watched her friends dance.

She bit her lip as she saw Lisa turn her head to smile at Scott. Part of her wanted to march right up to them and demand what exactly they were doing. How could Lisa even think about ditching Stevie's brother for another guy? How dare Scott move in on Alex's girlfriend?

But she knew that wouldn't accomplish anything useful, either. She just had to keep quiet and let her friends figure things out for themselves. Still, it was weird to think about Lisa and Scott being together, on a date, as a couple—at least for one evening.

But maybe that's all it'll turn out to be, Stevie thought. *Maybe Lisa and Alex will come to their senses soon and realize that they belong together. Until then, all I can do is wait and see. And appreciate what Phil and I have even more, of course.*

"Hey," Phil's voice came from behind her. He put his hand on her arm. "There you are."

Suddenly feeling very, very grateful, Stevie spun around and flung her arms around her boyfriend. She buried her face in his scratchy wool sport coat and squeezed him as tightly as she could, breathing in the familiar scent of the cologne she'd bought him on their last anniversary.

"Whoa!" Phil said, a little breathless. "What's up with you? I was only gone for like two minutes."

Stevie loosened her grip just enough to stand on tiptoes and kiss him on the nose. "Oh, nothing," she said, her throat feeling a little tight. "I'm just glad that we're here. Together."

Carole pursed her lips, concentrating carefully as she applied a fresh coat of Marvelous Mocha lipstick. Cam was standing in the line at the refreshment table, waiting to get them some punch, and Carole had taken the opportunity to duck into the rest room inside the CARL building to check her face. She wasn't used to wearing much makeup, and all evening she'd had sudden, panicky visions of herself walking around with lipstick smeared across her chin or huge raccoonlike smudges of mascara around her eyes. When she'd finally gotten a look in the mirror, she had been relieved. Although most of her lipstick had worn off, the rest of her face looked fine.

As she was recapping her lipstick, the door opened and Callie walked in. "Hi!" she greeted Carole with a smile. "Having fun?"

"Big time," Carole replied. "You?"

Callie nodded and pulled a tube of lip gloss out of her small evening bag. "It seems like the fund-raiser is a big success," she said, slicking the gloss onto her lips. "Everyone in town seems to be here." She glanced at Carole meaningfully. "Well, almost everyone," she amended. "I'll tell you, after that scene at school today, I was really glad that Veronica didn't show up."

Carole grimaced. She'd heard all about Stevie's confrontation with her old nemesis. "Me too," she agreed. "Though this would be an appropriate place for them to go another round. After all, they've always gotten along about as well as cats and dogs."

Callie chuckled. "So what's the deal with those two, anyway?" she asked, tossing her lip gloss back in her bag. "I mean, I know Veronica can be kind of hard to take. But Stevie seems to take her snobby attitude a lot more, I don't know, *personally* than most people do."

"I know." Carole leaned on the edge of the sink and sighed, thinking back over the years she'd known Stevie and Veronica. "They have a long history. I'm not sure what it is, but they just really rub each other the wrong way, and neither of them is very good at ignoring it." She glanced at Callie. "They used to be at each other's throats all the time when we were a little younger. Stevie was always pulling stunts like filling Veronica's boots with oats or getting her banned from the Starlight Ride. And Veronica would find equally mature ways to get back at her."

"Wow." Callie wrinkled her nose. "That must have kept things, um . . . interesting."

"I know." Carole sighed again. "Once Veronica stopped riding regularly and we all started high school, things cooled down and we all hoped that was the end of it. But now, with Stevie's article and then this gossip column thing . . . Well, I just hope it isn't the start of World War Three." Suddenly realizing that Cam was probably waiting for her by then, she excused herself and hurried out of the rest room. Stevie and Veronica would just have to sort out their problems for themselves. Carole, for one, had more interesting things to think about.

Stevie was munching on a cookie and watching the action on the dance floor, swaying slightly to the beat, when she felt a tap on her shoulder. When she turned, she saw Scott's grinning face. "Hey there, lover," he said, waggling his eyebrows suggestively.

Stevie felt her face flush. "So you know," she said flatly, realizing right away that there was no point in pretending she didn't know what Scott was talking about. "Who told you?"

Scott snorted. "Nobody had to tell me anything," he replied. "It was printed in the newspaper, remember?"

"Oh, yeah." Stevie shot him a sheepish look out of the corner of her eye, wondering if it was possible to be more embarrassed than she was at the moment. "Sorry about that. Looks like I was way off, huh?" She glanced around for Lisa, but she was nowhere in sight.

Scott patted her on the back. "Hey, it's no big deal," he insisted. "Actually, you're weren't that far off. I mean, I *was* hanging around the stable a lot trying to spend more time with Lisa, and that meant spending more time with her friends, too." He shrugged, looking slightly sheepish himself. "To be honest, I didn't even realize what I was doing at first. I wouldn't even admit to myself that I liked her until I heard about—" He shot Stevie a glance and abruptly changed directions. "Anyway, don't give yourself a hard time. I *am* crazy about you, you know. Just not in that way. In fact, I sort of think of you as part of the family. More like a sister than just another friend."

"Oh, great." Stevie rolled her eyes. "Just what I need. Another brother."

Scott laughed, and Stevie joined in. But inside, she felt a little weird.

Friend or not, I'm not sure I like having him confide in me about Lisa, she thought worriedly. *After all, Lisa and Alex are only broken up temporarily. They'll probably get back together before too much longer. And then where does that leave Scott?*

"I'll be right back," Scott said. "I'm just going to grab us some more punch."

Lisa nodded and smiled up at him from her seat on a folding chair at the edge of the dance floor. "I'll be right here," she replied lightly.

He rested one hand lightly on her shoulder for a moment, then turned and headed for the refreshment table. Lisa sat back in her chair and looked out over the scene, her gaze wandering to the small podium at the far end of the dance floor, where a maternal-looking woman with a big CARL button on her dress was adjusting a microphone. Behind the woman, Lisa spotted A.J., Callie, and a couple of other people she recognized petting a large, active Dalmatian and chatting with another CARL volunteer. Meanwhile, out on the floor, Stevie and Phil were dancing together, right alongside Carole and Cam.

Practically everyone I know is here except Alex, Lisa

thought, watching her friends. *It's weird, his not being here. And it's even weirder that I'm really okay with that. In fact, it's sort of a relief that he's not around tonight.*

Her mind wandered back to her mother's big announcement. She hadn't mentioned a word about it to Scott, but she knew that if she were with Alex that night, she would already have told him about it.

He would be even more upset about it than I am, she told herself with a grimace. *And that would make me feel even worse. Instead, I can just relax and try to forget about it—at least for one night.*

Thinking about Alex, she couldn't help wondering what he was doing that evening. Was he with Nicole? At the thought, Lisa felt a twinge of something that could have been jealousy. Then again, maybe it wasn't.

Scott returned a few minutes later with their drinks, just in time to take a seat beside her before the CARL volunteer tapped on the microphone and called for attention. "What's happening now?" Lisa murmured, sipping her punch.

"Looks like there's going to be a speaker," Scott said. "That's usually how these fund-raisers go. Get everyone relaxed and then remind them why they're really here."

Lisa nodded, shooting him a curious glance. With his family, attending charity fund-raisers was probably as ordinary an outing as going to the movies or the mall was for most people. It was a strange thought.

"Could I have your attention, please?" the woman at the microphone said. "Thank you. First of all, on behalf of all of us at the County Animal Rescue League—two-legged and four-legged alike—I wish to offer my heartfelt thanks to you for turning out in such numbers tonight."

A ragged cheer went up from the listeners. Lisa smiled as she noticed Stevie pumping her fist in the air.

"Now if you'll give me a few moments, I'd like to talk to you about our rescue mission here at CARL . . ."

That's what I *need,* Lisa thought idly as the woman continued speaking. *Someone to rescue me. From my messed-up family, from planning for college, from worrying about what's going on with me and Alex, and now from this new plan of Mom's.* She glanced over at Scott. His profile was sober, intent, and handsome as he listened to the volunteer's speech. *I wish someone could just swoop in and rescue me from all of it. . . .*

Carole couldn't remember the last time she'd had so much fun—outside a stable, at least. As she and Cam strolled hand in hand through the main hall in the CARL building, looking at the displays of photos that the volunteers had set up, she wished the wonderful evening would never end.

Maybe someday Cam and I will come back here to CARL together, she mused, pressing herself against his side as he stopped to pick up a brochure about vaccinations. *We'll have a stable together—it wouldn't even have to be a big, fancy one like I was daydreaming about the other day. It could just be a couple of horses in the backyard. That would be as wonderful as the fanciest farm full of Thoroughbreds, as long as it was ours together.*

She slipped her arm around Cam's waist as they moved on down the hall. He glanced at her with a smile, resting his arm on her shoulders.

Carole sighed contentedly and returned to her reverie. *Of course, even the smallest stable needs a few stable cats to keep the mice out of the feed,* she thought with a smile. *Cam and I could come here to pick some out. We could name them after our favorite places to go together—one could be called Magnolia, after our first date at the Magnolia Diner; another could be named Carl because of tonight; and of course one would have to be called Pine Hollow.* She almost giggled out loud at the thought of a cat named Pine Hollow, but she managed to control herself, suspecting that Cam might not understand her weird little daydream. *Anyway, we could also pick out a nice family dog while we were here,* she added with another happy sigh, imagining herself grooming Starlight in front of a tidy little three-stall barn while Cam played fetch nearby with their faithful pooch.

Cam paused in front of a poster showing some of the animals currently available for adoption at CARL. The kennel runs and cat rooms were locked up tight that night—Carole knew that the volunteers thought that having hundreds of people wandering around would be too much excitement for the animals. This way the guests could take a look at CARL's residents, and the animals themselves could get a good night's sleep.

"I wish Mom and Dad would let me get a dog," Cam remarked. He pointed to a photo of a large black dog with a snub nose and an alert expression. "This one looks cool. What do you think?"

Carole shrugged. "I guess," she said uncertainly. "I usually like smaller dogs myself. Like Lisa's old Lhasa apso, Dolly. Or the Regnerys' puppy, Mulligan—she's a pug."

Cam wrinkled his nose. "Small dogs?" he teased. "Small dogs are for wimps. If we ever came in here looking for a dog together, I'd talk you into a Great Dane before you knew it."

Did he just say what I think he said? Carole thought in amazement. It sounded as if Cam had been having some of the same kinds of thoughts as she had! Realizing that they'd both been imagining a future together made her feel closer to him than ever. She wasn't sure whether to throw him against the wall and kiss him or break into tears of sheer happiness. Instead, she decided to play along.

"A Great Dane? No way," she said with mock disgust. "We're getting a Chihuahua."

Cam laughed. "Are you kidding? Starlight would step on it!" he exclaimed. He turned toward her, encircling her waist with his arms. "I think we may have to compromise here. How do you feel about medium-sized dogs?"

Carole smiled up at him. She could hardly believe that this was really her life—that Cam was really her boyfriend. She'd felt so left out for so long, but now her love life was on track at last. And it had definitely been worth waiting for.

"Medium-sized dogs are perfect," she murmured as she tilted her face up to receive Cam's kiss.

Lisa's house was dark when Scott pulled into her driveway—except for the faint glow of the front hall lamp, which Mrs. Atwood always left on when she went to bed before Lisa got home.

"Wow, I guess it's later than I realized," Scott commented, glancing at the darkened house and then at his watch as he turned off the car. "Time flies when you're having a wonderful time with a wonderful person."

"Mom goes to bed pretty early these days," Lisa began before realizing what he'd just said. "Oh! But I had a nice time, too. A really nice time."

She glanced over at him shyly, realizing it was true. *You know, a week ago I wouldn't have believed it was possible for me to enjoy myself at a dance without Alex,* she thought. *But I really did have fun with Scott.*

Once again, Scott hurried around to help Lisa out of the car. Then he walked her up the front walk. Soon they reached the front step, and Lisa paused there, fumbling for her keys before turning to smile shyly at Scott. "Well . . . thanks," she said softly, unable to avoid noticing how handsome he looked in the spillover from the streetlamps.

Scott gazed down at her, his expression unreadable in the near darkness. "Believe me," he said huskily, "the pleasure is entirely mine."

Lisa gulped, suddenly feeling awkward. This was the moment she'd always dreaded on first dates in the past—the moment when she waited to see whether the guy was going to kiss her good night. Even through the first few weeks with Alex, she'd always felt an anxious pang when the end of the evening rolled around. He'd been nervous and uncertain and goofy, usually catching her in the middle of a sentence or bumping her nose with his own.

Scott didn't leave her in suspense for long. Taking a step toward her, he gently grasped her chin in one hand and tilted her face up slightly. His other arm slipped around her back as he bent and kissed her, his lips surprisingly soft and gentle.

Lisa was startled at the intense feeling that suddenly rushed through her as she returned his kiss, her hands automatically moving to encircle his waist. She never would have expected that kissing Scott would feel so *good*.

She jumped away suddenly, gasping slightly for breath. "Um, so, good night," she said, feeling flustered and a little bit spooked.

Scott didn't seem to mind the sudden end to their kiss. "Good night, Lisa," he said softly. "I'll talk to you tomorrow."

Lisa stared after him as he strolled down the walk and climbed into his car. She didn't turn to head inside until long after his car's taillights had disappeared at the end of the block. *What just happened here?* she wondered, still feeling a little breathless and unbalanced. *What exactly just happened here?*

FIFTEEN

"Would you stop grinning like that?" Callie told Scott, glancing at him across the breakfast table the next morning. "It's irritating to see someone so cheerful so early."

Scott shrugged, his grin widening. "Sorry. Can't help it. I'm a happy guy."

Callie snorted, though she wasn't really annoyed with him. She was just tired—it had been pretty late when Stevie and Phil had dropped her off after the CARL party. But she hadn't wanted to sleep in, since she'd planned to spend all morning at Pine Hollow training on one of Max's horses. There was no telling when she might find the right horse to buy, and in the meantime she wanted to keep herself in shape.

"Are you almost ready?" she asked her brother, standing up to carry her cereal bowl to the sink.

Scott nodded and stood as well, helping her clear the table and then leading the way out to the front hall. He paused in the doorway to the den, where their parents were lounging on the sofa reading the newspaper and drinking coffee. "We're off," he announced.

Congressman Forester looked up. "So long, kids," he said. "Have fun."

"Thanks, Dad." Callie grabbed her coat from the closet and swung open the front door. She started to step out onto the porch, stopping herself just in time to avoid tripping over a large, festively wrapped package nestled against the threshold. She frowned at it in surprise. It was much too early for the mail to have arrived. Someone must have dropped it off personally.

Scott peered over her shoulder. "What's that?"

"I don't know." Callie leaned over to get a better look. She gulped. "It has my name on it." Who would leave her a big, fancy gift like that?

No, she thought as one possibility floated into her mind. *He wouldn't . . .*

"Dad?" Scott called. "You'd better come check this out."

"Shhh!" Callie hissed in annoyance. The last thing she wanted was to broadcast her surprise early Christmas gift to the whole family. "You don't need to—"

It was too late. "What is it?" their father asked, pushing Scott aside and glancing out at the porch. "Oh. I see. Come back inside, kids."

"But Dad!" Callie protested, glancing at her watch. "It's—"

"Now, Callie," he repeated in the stern voice he usually saved for his toughest congressional opponents. "Go sit down with your mother. I'm calling the police."

"The police?" Callie cried. "But we were just on our way to—"

"Sit," her father thundered, already grabbing the nearest phone and punching in numbers. Soon he was talking to a detective, describing the package. ". . . and the only identifying mark is my daughter's name written on a tag," he finished. "Yes, I think that's a good idea. Thank you."

"What did he say?" Mrs. Forester asked her husband.

Congressman Forester hung up the phone and glanced at her. "They're sending the bomb squad."

Callie's jaw dropped. *"What?"*

Her father sighed and rubbed his jaw, glancing nervously toward the still open front door. "I'm afraid we can't take any chances," he said heavily. "The papers have been having a field day with this new welfare controversy, and there are some pretty strong feelings on both sides. And my name is on the pending legislation, so . . ." He ended with a shrug. "Come on. I think we'd better wait for the police in the backyard."

The next forty minutes were like some kind of bad made-for-TV movie, at least as far as Callie was concerned. As she and Scott stood around watching, police swarmed into the house, taking notes and stomping around and generally being very deferential to Congressman Forester. Soon after the first cars arrived, a van pulled up, and several large German shepherds jumped out. After the dogs had sniffed the package for a while, a bomb specialist carefully approached it, dressed in so much protective gear that he looked ready to walk on the moon rather than the Foresters' porch. He carried the package to the middle of the backyard, near the pool. Then he poked and prodded and finally unwrapped the package while everyone else stood well back and watched.

He opened the box contained in the wrapping and peered inside. Then he pushed his safety mask back and stood up. "It's okay," he called. "It's clean."

"Whew!" Mrs. Forester exclaimed. "Thank you so much, officers. Now, if you'd all like a cup of coffee . . . ?" She led the way toward the back of the house, drawing the police officer behind her like the Pied Piper.

Callie's father paused as he started to follow. "Sorry about that, sweetie," he said, putting his arm around her shoulders for a quick hug. "But you really ought to tell your friends that surprises might not be such a good idea from now on."

Callie grimaced, not bothering to respond. Her father was already hurrying after the other adults, anyway. Soon only she and Scott were left in the backyard. "Well?" Scott prompted. "After all that, aren't you going to check it out?"

"I guess," Callie muttered, half wishing that the bomb squad had just blown up the package, like she'd heard they sometimes did with suspicious packages at the airport. She walked over to the box, which was lying in the grass among the remains of its wrapping paper and ribbon, and squatted beside it. "It's from The Saddlery," she commented as she picked it up.

She lifted the lid and peeled back the tissue paper inside. Beneath, she saw a mass of wool tweed. She lifted it and shook it out and finally recognized what the item was. A coat. A formal riding coat—tweedy and traditional, not Callie's style at all. After all the hoopla, it was almost laughable. Almost.

"Hmmm," Scott said, blinking at the coat in surprise. "That's . . . nice, I guess."

Yeah, nice *is definitely the word,* Callie thought, stuffing it back in the box. *It's nice and conservative— the kind of thing Lisa might wear, but not me.*

"Come on, let's get over to the stable," she told Scott, standing up abruptly and tucking the box under her arm, planning to shove it in the front closet on her way past. "We're late as it is."

Scott raised one eyebrow. "But who—"

"Just come on." Callie didn't feel like discussing it. Even though there had been no name on the card other than her own, she knew that there was only one person in the world who could have left her such an inappropriate, ridiculous, unwanted gift.

She just didn't know what to do about it.

When Lisa arrived at Pine Hollow on Saturday morning, the first person she saw was Ben Marlow. She had just stepped into the entryway, shaking off the cold—it was the briskest morning yet, making it feel like Christmas—when he emerged from the indoor ring pushing a wheelbarrow full of manure. Lisa noticed vaguely that he looked kind of glum, but that was no breaking news bulletin. Ben almost always looked glum.

She nodded politely and took a few steps toward the locker room. Ben cleared his throat. "Lisa," he said.

Lisa stopped short in surprise. Until that moment she hadn't been positive that Ben even knew her name. She couldn't remember him ever using it before. "Yes?" she said, turning to face him. "What is it, Ben?"

He coughed, not quite meeting her eye. "Uh, I just—I wanted to ask—" He broke off, obviously struggling for words. "Never mind," he muttered, turning quickly and pushing the wheelbarrow off toward the stable aisle.

Lisa blinked and watched him go. Then, shaking her head, she continued toward the locker room. She had bigger things on her mind that day than Ben Marlow's usual weird behavior.

Even before she reached the locker room, she heard the sounds of voices and laughter. Stepping inside, she saw that Carole was perched on the bench in front of the cubbies, chatting with Stevie, who was pulling on her boots. Callie was digging around inside her cubby, while Scott leaned casually against the wall near the door.

Scott. Lisa blushed when she saw him. She still hadn't decided what to think about their date the night before, or about him.

Stevie was the first to notice her entrance. "Yo, Lisa!" she called cheerfully.

Carole and Callie added their greetings. But Scott took it a step further.

"Hi," he said, his face lighting up when he looked at her. Standing up straight, he stepped over the bench and came toward her. "We were just wondering when you'd get here."

Before Lisa could respond, he'd reached her and put a hand on her arm, leaning over and giving her a quick kiss on the cheek. Lisa was so startled that she couldn't say a word for a moment. "Um, I'm here," she managed lamely at last.

Scott smiled down at her. "I had a really great time with you last night," he said in a low voice. "I hope we can do it again sometime."

Lisa blushed deeper than ever, embarrassed that their conversation was taking place in front of an audience, especially since she wasn't even sure how she felt about Scott. Then she happened to glance at Stevie, whose face was pink. Suddenly she remembered Stevie's theory about why Scott was hanging around Pine Hollow so much, and a giggle escaped before she could stop it.

"What?" Scott looked startled. "Was it something I said?"

"No, no, I'm sorry," Lisa said hastily, grinning in Stevie's direction. "It's something somebody else said. Somebody in this room, actually."

Stevie scowled at her. "Oh, go ahead and say it," she said crossly. "It's not like everybody here doesn't already know, anyway. You're laughing at me."

Lisa giggled again, and soon everybody was laughing, Stevie included. Stevie even walked over and gave Scott a big, wet kiss on the cheek, reminding Lisa once again why she liked Stevie so much. She really was a pretty good sport.

Well, most of the time, anyway, Lisa amended. *As long as Veronica isn't involved.*

She was distracted from that thought by a flash of movement outside the room. Glancing over, she saw Ben walking by, his hands in his pockets and his gaze directed into the room. Following his intense stare, Lisa realized that his eyes were locked on Carole.

Guess he finally realized she wouldn't wait around for him forever, she thought dismissively. *His loss.*

She didn't spend much time feeling sorry for him.

Ben was a big boy, and Lisa had her own problems to worry about.

She shuddered as she remembered her mother's excited chatter at breakfast that morning about calling a real estate agent and putting their house on the market. *And the list is getting longer all the time,* she added grimly.

"Do you want to ride Checkers today?" Carole asked Cam, already reaching for the roan gelding's bridle. "I think you'd like him."

"Hey!" Lisa protested. "I was going to ride Checkers."

"No way, I'm the guest," Cam said with a grin and a wink for Carole.

She giggled. "He has a point, Lisa."

Stevie snorted, glancing up from hoisting Belle's saddle. "Yeah, right. You'd say that if he'd just declared that horses should be allowed to vote." She paused for a second and considered what she'd just said. "Of course, you'd probably agree with that no matter who said it."

Carole blushed as the others laughed, including Cam. But before she could defend herself, there was a loud whoop from the office next door.

"What was that?" Lisa asked in surprise.

A second later Max stuck his head into the room. "Guess what?" he cried, grinning from ear to ear. "I just hired our new stable hand! She starts Monday—just in time to help out with the Starlight Ride."

Carole noticed Max winking at Stevie, but she didn't even bother to wonder what that was all about. She was too busy dealing with her own feelings of surprise, apprehension, and, yes, jealousy. A new stable hand? She couldn't help being disturbed at the idea of someone new working at Pine Hollow while she herself was still on probation. She'd known it was coming—Max had made no secret of the fact that he was looking to hire more help—but the announcement that it was really happening still came as a shock.

She was still thinking about it as she and Cam rode out of the stable yard together a short while later. "Penny for your thoughts," Cam said after a moment.

"What?" Carole smiled self-consciously, realizing that she'd hardly said a word to him for several minutes. "Oh, sorry. I was just thinking about Max's announcement. It's weird to think about someone new coming to Pine Hollow. Things changing. You know."

Cam gave her an understanding look. "Don't worry," he said, steering Checkers around a dip in the field they were crossing. "Max isn't trying to replace you." He smiled. "That would be impossible."

"Thanks. And I know." Carole shot him a grateful look. "It's just weird, that's all. Mostly because it still feels weird not to have a job here anymore."

"Well, think about it this way," Cam said. "Not

having a job means you have more time for the finer things in life. Like spending time with me." He shot her a rakish grin.

Carole laughed. "Okay, you're right. That *is* a silver lining," she said. Her laughter faded quickly as she recalled Max's comment about the new person starting in time for the Starlight Ride. "Still, this is usually my favorite time of year at Pine Hollow," she added wistfully. "I hate to think I'll probably miss the Starlight Ride." She leaned forward to pat her horse, thinking back to that special night when she'd first realized he was hers.

Cam nodded, watching her. "Yes, I've been thinking about that," he said pensively. "And I've decided there's just one solution. I'm going to work on your father between now and then—convince him to let you go with me."

Carole raised an eyebrow. "I don't know," she began. "Dad's not the easily convinced type."

"I know. But I think he likes me." He shrugged. "Besides, he knows how important that night is to you—it's when he gave you Starlight, right? So all I have to do is drop a few hints, remind him of that . . ."

"Oh. I guess it's worth a shot." Carole thought the plan sounded a little sneaky, but she didn't say so. If he could actually convince her father to let her go, who was she to complain about his methods? He had only the best of intentions—he wanted her to be happy, and he wanted them to have a nice, romantic Christmas Eve together.

They didn't speak again until they reached the woods. As they entered the shady trail that led down to the creek, Cam glanced over at her. "Can we stop for a sec?" he asked. "I think Checkers may have picked up a stone."

"Of course!" Carole pulled up Starlight immediately, glancing at the other horse's feet with concern. She waited as Cam slid out of the saddle and picked up the roan gelding's right fore, leaning over it. "Well?" she called expectantly. "Do you see anything?"

"I'm not sure," Cam called back. "Could you come take a look?"

Carole frowned slightly. It hadn't been that long since Cam had been picking out his horse's feet. Had he already forgotten what a stone looked like? But she swung down from her saddle, leaving Starlight ground-tied on the trail.

She hurried around to join Cam, who had dropped Checkers's foot. "Let me see," she said, bending over to pick up the foot again.

Before she could do so, Cam grabbed her around the waist. "Forget it," he said, pulling her to him. "There's no stone. It was all a cruel hoax."

Carole blinked. "Huh?"

Cam grinned at her expression of surprise. "I made up that story about the stone," he said, holding her close. "I just wanted to get you on the ground so that I could do this." He kissed her, his arms tightening around her.

They didn't break apart until Checkers snorted loudly and swung his head around, nudging curiously at Carole's back. With a giggle, Carole pulled away. "I think he's trying to tell us something," she said.

Cam gazed down at her, his dark eyes locked on her own. "Well, there's something I want to tell you, too," he said, ignoring the horse. "That's the other reason I tricked you into dismounting. I wanted to be able to look into your eyes when I said it."

"What is it, Cam?" Carole asked with a flash of fear. He looked so serious. Was he going to tell her it was over? Was her happiness going to be so short-lived? "Go ahead," she said as bravely as she could. "I'm ready."

"I know we've only been together for a week," Cam said softly, taking both her hands in his. "That's not much time. But it's enough for me to know how I feel about you. And I don't believe in wasting time—not when it comes to something this important." He took a deep breath. "That's why I want to tell you now. I love you, Carole Hanson."

Carole was stunned. Her jaw dropped, and for a moment her mind went blank. Was this really happening? What was she supposed to say now?

Finally she figured it out. The past week had been

the most wonderful week she could remember. And it was all thanks to Cam. So there was really only one thing she could say.

"I love you too, Cam Nelson." This time when he bent down to kiss her, Carole knew that it would take much more than a nudge from an impatient horse to break them apart.

ABOUT THE AUTHOR

BONNIE BRYANT is the author of more than a hundred books about horses, including the Pine Hollow series, The Saddle Club series, The Saddle Club Super Editions, and the Pony Tails series. She has also written novels and movie novelizations under her married name, B. B. Hiller.

Ms. Bryant began writing The Saddle Club in 1986. Although she had done some riding before that, she intensified her studies then and found herself learning right along with her characters Stevie, Carole, and Lisa. She claims that they are all much better riders than she is.

Ms. Bryant was born and raised in New York City. She still lives there, in Greenwich Village, with her two sons.